HD

St. Helens Libraries

Please return / renew this item by the last date shown.
Books may be renewed by phone and Internet.

Telephone - (01744) 676954 or 677822
Email - centrallibrary@sthelens.gov.uk
Online - sthelens.gov.uk/librarycatalogue
Twitter - twitter.com/STHLibraries

G2- AUG 2016   G18
K11 -- DEC 2016
M17 -- APR 2017
Q8
C21 - MAR 2018
M3   -- AUG 2017
Q14 -- OCT 2018
E22 -- MAY 2018
D9 -- CC

KU-545-085

SPECIAL MESSAGE TO READERS

THE ULVERSCROFT FOUNDATION
(registered UK charity number 264873)
was established in 1972 to provide funds for research, diagnosis and treatment of eye diseases.
Examples of major projects funded by the Ulverscroft Foundation are:-

- The Children's Eye Unit at Moorfields Eye Hospital, London
- The Ulverscroft Children's Eye Unit at Great Ormond Street Hospital for Sick Children
- Funding research into eye diseases and treatment at the Department of Ophthalmology, University of Leicester
- The Ulverscroft Vision Research Group, Institute of Child Health
- Twin operating theatres at the Western Ophthalmic Hospital, London
- The Chair of Ophthalmology at the Royal Australian College of Ophthalmologists

You can help further the work of the Foundation by making a donation or leaving a legacy.
Every contribution is gratefully received. If you would like to help support the Foundation or require further information, please contact:

THE ULVERSCROFT FOUNDATION
The Green, Bradgate Road, Anstey
Leicester LE7 7FU, England
Tel: (0116) 236 4325

website: www.foundation.ulverscroft.com

ALTERED IMAGES

When Cherry Hawthorn is told her image isn't right to promote the television show she invented, she decides to have a makeover. Thrilled when her dishy boss Alan Jenkins not only approves, but also promises to take the new her on a date, she sets off to Sea View Spa. There, she meets the friendly, scruffy, eccentric Edward Cameron, who immediately takes a shine to her. But can this bear of a man compete with Alan's smooth charm?

Books by Louise Armstrong
in the Linford Romance Library:

HOLD ON TO PARADISE
JAPANESE MAGIC
A PICTURE OF HAPPINESS
THE PRICE OF HAPPINESS
CONCRETE PROPOSAL
PATTERN OF LOVE
KINGFISHER DAYS
MASTER OF DIPLOMACY
HER GUARDIAN ANGEL
LOVE'S GAMBLE

LOUISE ARMSTRONG

◆

ALTERED IMAGES

Complete and Unabridged

LINFORD
Leicester

First published in Great Britain in 2015

First Linford Edition
published 2016

A catalogue record for this book is available
from the British Library.

ISBN 978–1–4448–2872–6

Published by
F. A. Thorpe (Publishing)
Anstey, Leicestershire

Set by Words & Graphics Ltd.
Anstey, Leicestershire
Printed and bound in Great Britain by
T. J. International Ltd., Padstow, Cornwall

This book is printed on acid-free paper

1

Cherry Hawthorn didn't enjoy working late, but she did enjoy the quiet of her office at nine o'clock at night. The company she worked for, Prize Television, had followed the example of ITV and the BBC by locating its offices in Media City, Manchester, and Cherry's windows overlooked Salford Quays.

Her colleagues had gone home. She'd been working for two hours with no interruptions. It was time for her to stand up, stretch, and snap off the main lights so she could enjoy the view from the floor-to-ceiling plate-glass window. It was just beginning to go dark on this fine June evening. The bridge over the canal glittered with lights. The Lowry theatre was lit up and beautiful, and a single swan floated over the black water, breaking up the light reflections into a shimmering V-shape of multi-coloured ripples.

Cherry turned away from the window and eyed the mound of work on her desk. A task lamp illuminated the tottering pile of papers. The mountain of work was shrinking, no doubt about it, but she was going to have to put in a serious amount of overtime if she were to clear her desk before leaving for the summer television show at Cannes next week. It was worth putting in overtime in order to attend such a glamorous event, she decided. And she couldn't wait to see what an international audience would make of the television show that she'd invented.

She smiled as she thought of the format. *Pony Princesses* had been horribly expensive to film — and her boss had had to promote the idea for her, because no one would take a risk on producing a game dreamed up by a woman with no track record — but by drawing on her own childhood passions, she'd come up with a game show for girls that involved ponies and pink outfits, and it was showing every sign of being the smash hit of the year.

She stretched, returned to her desk, and opened a pack of corn chips to keep her going. She dug out a jar of salsa to dip the chips into. It smelled delicious and tasted better. She remembered that there was sour cream in the fridge in the office kitchen, so fetched it and added a generous dollop to the feast. She'd probably be too tired to stop for dinner on the way home, so it wouldn't matter if she had a snack now.

She felt good about the quantity of work she'd already tackled. It was great to be able to get her head down. During the day, the office was so busy that work came in faster than she could file it in her in-tray, the phone rang constantly and people popped in every two minutes. This silence was bliss.

The door flew open at that very

moment, but the interruption didn't annoy her at all, because in walked five feet ten inches of perfection: her utterly desirable boss, Alan Jenkins. It was no surprise that he turned Cherry's knees to water: every woman in the building had a crush on the handsome Head of Department. He was just so good-looking. Although he was as English as they came, and had been to an ordinary school, there was a touch of the Ivy League about him. He cultivated the 'I'm-off-to-a-polo-match-the-minute-I've-finished-rowing' look. He favoured crisp Oxford shirts, blazers with gold buttons and cricket sweaters slung around his shoulders at just the right angle. There was some debate as to how he maintained a glowing tan in rainy old Manchester, and his streaked blond hair was too pretty to be one hundred percent natural, but no one could say that the effort he spent on grooming was wasted. He was one gorgeous man.

He flashed his perfect white teeth at her now.

'It's dark in here. I thought every-body had gone home. Are you burning the midnight oil?'

'Yes,' she replied, blushing. Why could she never act naturally around this man? 'I want to clear my desk before leaving for the television festival.'

The brilliant blue eyes shifted to one side. Then he cleared his throat.

'Ah, well, yes. We need to have a conversation about arrangements for Cannes.'

Cherry sighed, and then said, 'Hasn't Cherish managed to arrange our tickets yet?'

Given that administration jobs in television were so hotly sought after — she'd broken into the business that way herself — she was constantly amazed by how utterly useless nearly all the secretaries were. More than once she'd been glad that she, unlike some of her peers, could roll up her sleeves and organise things for herself if the administration failed.

'I'll see to it tomorrow,' she said,

scribbling on a pad. 'Travel arrangements don't seem to be in Cherish's skill set.'

But instead of accepting her offer gratefully, Alan shifted his weight, and rubbed one gleaming moccasin against the toe of his other fine leather shoe.

'There's no need to sort anything out. I have my tickets.'

'I don't have mine.'

'That's what I wanted to talk to you about. It's an issue relating to budget cuts. It may not be possible to find the funding to take you to France.'

Cherry stared at his face. His blue eyes wouldn't meet hers and he looked uncomfortable.

'It's not down to budget cuts,' she said slowly, feeling puzzled. 'You forget, Cherish was off sick last week. I took the minutes at the finance meeting. Travel and expenses were approved for two people. There is plenty of money! Of course I'm coming to the trade fair. The *Pony Princesses* programme is my responsibility! I have to do all I can to make it successful.'

Alan looked even more uncomfortable.

'It slipped my mind that you'd been present at the finance meeting.'

'Alan, what's happening here?'

He took a deep breath.

'I didn't want to share this information with you.' And now he did look at her. His blue eyes met hers with a blazing intensity that made her feel nervous. 'I didn't want to cause you any hurt.'

'What kind of hurt?'

'There is no easy way to say this. You won't be attending the trade festival.'

Cherry was pretty easy-going, but *Pony Princesses* was her baby. She fired up at once.

'You can't leave me behind! I have to make sure *Pony Princesses* does well. It's my first ever programme, you know important it is!'

'You seem to forget how much of the development and production work was entirely my effort — '

'You only had to take the idea to meetings! You know that nobody would listen to me — '

He held up a hand to stop her.

'Cherry, Cherry, Cherry! There is no point in arguing because ownership is not the issue. Of course it's your programme. The problem lies in another area entirely.'

'You'll have to tell me what the problem is.'

'I'm sorry, but you are forcing me to discuss matters that we agreed it would be better to keep from you.'

'We?' she queried.

Alan waved his hand in the air as if her question was a troublesome fly that that he were brushing aside.

'Oh, certain people in management, and the people in Human Resources. We care about you, Cherry, and so we decided that it was better for you if you didn't represent the company at Cannes.'

'I don't understand. Why, why are people talking about me behind my back — holding meetings about me, even? What's going on?'

For one horrible moment Cherry wondered if she were getting the sack. Alan took a step towards her and put his hand on her shoulder. She was too upset to be thrilled by the contact. In fact, she felt queasy as a wave of heavy aftershave hit her nostrils.

'Tell me straight!' she demanded. 'Why don't people want me to go to Cannes?'

Alan looked at her and shook his head. His blue eyes were full of pity and concern.

'Television is a very shallow business,' he remarked. 'I wish it were different, but we have to deal with reality. Image is ultra-important; and, well, Cherry, your image . . . I don't have to spell it out for you, do I?'

Cherry looked at the far wall of the office. She could see their reflections in the floor-to-ceiling dark glass. They shimmered because her hazel eyes were full of tears, but she could still see the contrast between the figures. One tall slender man in a crisp blue shirt; one small — and, it had to be admitted, roly-poly — woman in black.

She knew what he was talking about, all right; she just hadn't had to deal with comments about her looks since she'd left the teasing of school behind her. One of the best things about being grown-up and working in television was that everyone she met was too kind, or too careful, to ever mention her size. Nobody ever called her fat. It was true that Alan had teased her one day when he'd caught her tucking into fish and chips, but he'd been so kind and caring when he'd realised that he had upset her that she'd been thrilled by his attention; and he'd never mentioned her weight again — until today.

She was twenty-six now, and she'd been lulled into a false sense of security. Her looks had ceased to bother her. She avoided men socially, and she didn't date; but, surrounded by politically-correct people who never reminded her that she wasn't thin, she'd come to think that how one looked wasn't important. She'd come to believe that in the world of work it was your brains that mattered, and she knew that her brains were more than good enough. She was doing well in her chosen career.

School had been such torture that she'd left as soon as the law allowed. Knowing that she wanted to work in television, she'd hatched her plans and pursued them with energy, and been rewarded by success. Secretarial skills had landed her a temporary position at the television studios. Hard work had turned that into a permanent position. Even harder work had led to the difficult jump from administration into the programme development team, and now her first programme looked like being a success. It had all been going so well, until today.

'I know how you must feel,' Alan said, speaking softly. He squeezed her shoulder, then gave her a couple of pats. 'I've never forgotten that day you confided in me. I'd have given anything to spare you this conversation.'

Only an hour ago, Cherry would have been thrilled by his attention. How many of her fantasies had begun with them alone in this very room with the lights dim and no one else around? And now he was touching her, just the way she'd dreamed of, but she was too churned up inside to enjoy it.

'Nobody's going to look at me!' she cried passionately. 'Even if they do, I don't care. I care about my programme, that's all.'

Alan shook his head.

'I'm sorry, we can't allow it. Management won't take the chance.'

'What chance?' Cherry demanded.

'We have a duty to protect our employees. Another episode like the one with Sandra Gilligan could be very damaging to our reputation.'

Emotions churned inside Cherry, and she wished she could think clearly so she could find the words that would change Alan's mind. She wished, too, that the horrible sinking feeling inside her heart that was telling her that she was wasting her time would go away, but her instincts persisted in telling her she was beaten.

'Sandra is nearly better,' Cherry tried. 'I hear she'll be back at work next month. Honestly, Alan, our situations are nothing alike.'

Poor, vulnerable, brilliant Sandra, she thought. The Internet campaign against the comedian had been vicious, and based solely on her weight and appearance. She'd been ridiculed in the press for appearing at an awards ceremony in a dress that had made people laugh for all the wrong reasons. And then, just like a gang forming in the changing rooms at school, the public had joined in, sending hateful texts and tweets, until Sandra had been driven into a nervous breakdown.

A crease was forming between Alan's eyebrows.

'Even if Sandra comes back tomorrow, she has still cost us a year's absence, and some extremely expensive counselling. In these testing times, the department cannot support continual drains on its resources.'

'Sandra is famous, and she has the artistic temperament. I'm ordinary, and people don't know who I am,' Cherry argued frantically. 'I can't imagine who would be bothered to send an internet message about me!'

'It's all settled. As a department, as a company, we can't afford to take the risk. We care about our staff and have a duty to protect them.'

And Cherry knew she was beaten. She'd already found out that if the risk assessment said no, the company wouldn't budge. They didn't want negative publicity. They didn't want lawsuits. And maybe, just maybe, they did care a little bit about their staff. In any case, it was all settled. She was barred from attending the trade show. She ran frantic fingers through her blonde hair and tugged hard at the curly locks.

'I have to go to the show and the festival. My career will go no further if I don't.'

Alan shrugged. She felt the motion run through his arm and down to the hand that was still on her shoulder. My goodness! He was so close to her still. They were still alone! She'd never had his undivided attention for so long . . . but she'd never imagined it happening in this upsetting situation. *Be careful what you wish for*, she told herself with a flash of her usual good humour.

Alan dropped his hand, and made getting-ready-to-leave movements.

'I mustn't keep you.'

'I have time to spare if I'm not going to France. I don't need to rush through this work now,' Cherry pointed out in what was meant to be a light voice. To her dismay, there was a distinct wobble in it.

Her career! Her precious, precious

career! It was her life. This could not be allowed to happen.

'First thing in the morning, I'm going to speak with the people in Human Resources,' she cried.

Alan nipped smartly back to her side and placed an arm around her shoulder.

'I assure you that the decision cannot be overturned. The only outcome of trying to reopen the matter would be hurt and upset for you, Cherry, and that's not what I want for you.'

It was the closest he'd ever been to her, but Cherry met the concern in his blue eyes without a single thrill. She was too upset about her career.

'I must try to persuade them to let me go to the trade show. I'll never succeed if the company won't let me network!'

Alan drew her to him.

'You can rely on me to promote your work for you.'

'Thank you,' Cherry replied, but it was an automatic response.

16

Her brain was busy. She had never thought about her looks as a problem to be solved, but she was used to plotting and planning when it came to her career. It was only a few seconds before the answer popped fully-formed into her mind. If her size and appearance were a problem, then she would change them.

'I'll go on a diet,' she cried.

Alan's gaze flicked to the corn chips that lay scattered across Cherry's desk like drifts of autumn leaves, the pools of dripping red salsa, and the dribbling carton of white cream. Then he smiled and hugged her.

'That's an excellent idea, Cherry. I'm glad that you realise that the way forward is entirely within your domain.'

Cherry's rational thought was taking wing and flying away. This was unreal! She was in Alan Jenkins's arms! He was hugging her! Now she had an answer to her problem, she could enjoy it! Cherry lifted her head to look up into that handsome, smiling tanned face.

'I believe in your ability to succeed,' he told her, and the gleam in his blue eyes warned her that he was going to make a move of some kind. Her ears buzzed and a flash of pleasure began to scramble what was left of her brains.

He drew one fingertip over the curve of her cheek and smiled in a way that blew her common sense straight out of the window. She gazed yearningly into Alan's handsome face. She was swooning like the heroine in a black-and-white movie. He looked down at her and smiled.

'The prospect of a new you excites me. It could move our relationship onto a new plane — that is, if you'd be interested in spending time with me when I get back.'

'I'd love to,' she squeaked.

His white teeth flashed in a smile.

'I'll look forward to our new, and beautiful, relationship.'

Then he put a fingertip under Cherry's chin and tilted it so that she had to look up at him. His blue eyes examined her face. He seemed to be satisfied by what he saw there.

'Promise that you'll put yourself 'on hold' for me?'

He continued to to look at her, waiting for an answer. He still sounded, and looked, like a movie star. Cherry felt her grip on reality slipping. She'd dreamed about a moment like this for months, and now it was happening, she couldn't believe it. She couldn't speak.

'Cherry?' he questioned, taking her by the shoulders and giving her a little shake. 'Is there someone else? Please don't disappoint me.'

'There's no one else,' she managed to say, and pride made her add: 'Not at the moment.'

Surely he knew that she'd never been on a proper date in all of the twenty-six years she'd been on this planet. Why should the next two weeks be any different?

'Promise!' he insisted. 'It's important to me.'

His words made her knees tremble.

19

'OK,' she managed to say.

He touched a lock of her hair, and then smoothed it behind her ear in a gesture that should have been charming.

'The upside of the situation is that your leave is booked from tomorrow, so you now have two free weeks. Why don't you take the opportunity to work on your idea for a knitting competition format? I thought the notion had distinct potential. I'll make you a deal. Before I leave, I'll book a table for our first date at The Correspondent's Club, and then you can impress me by having a brilliant new programme that we can discuss as we eat.'

The Correspondent's Club was Manchester's newest and most popular destination for writers and actors. It was smart, it was expensive, and it was full of media folk. If Alan was taking her to such a public restaurant, he was serious about having a relationship with her.

'Alan, I'd love that!'

He whipped out his electronic organiser and made a note.

'Are you free on June the twenty-seventh?'

Cherry made a pretence of checking her own diary, but in her secret heart she knew there wasn't an appointment in the world that would keep her from a date with Alan Jenkins.

'It should be OK,' she said, with a casualness she was rather proud of.

He touched her face again, and his lips stretched in a toothpaste smile.

'Good! I'll be looking forward to our first date the whole time I'm away.'

Then he did turn and leave her. Cherry watched his departing back, knowing that he'd turn in the doorway for a parting remark. He never left a room without looking back and making a comment. Sure enough, he turned and smiled at her.

'You might want to think about getting some exercise during your holiday. It's not going to be easy to lose so much weight.'

2

It wasn't easy to find a health spa at three days' notice, but finally Cherry tracked down a setup in Blackpool that had one place left. The photos on the website made the place look run-down and seedy, and she was about to flick past, but a huge red banner popped up saying: 'Under New Management: phone for great deals!'

It's not far from Manchester, and I'm desperate, she reminded herself, and reached for the phone.

'I don't want to mislead you,' the owner explained in a brisk voice. 'I have only just bought this spa and makeover business, and there's still a lot about the building that I need to improve. On the other hand, I promise I'll do my best to resolve any problems that may crop up; and, of course, I'm offering my first guests a substantial reduction.'

'Thank goodness she is dropping the price! I couldn't afford it otherwise!' Cherry thought, bug-eyed at the astronomical figure required to stay in a crumbling hotel and eat nothing for two weeks. She paid it, though. It was worth any amount of money to solve all her problems, she thought as she packed.

The hotel, when she finally found it, looked a thousand times worse than in its photographs. The building was so dingy from the outside that she drove past it twice, sure that there must be another 'Seaview Spa' nearby. Finally admitting that this peeling grey wreck had to be her destination, she pulled up on the other side side of the road, stared sadly at the tattered hulk and shook her head in disbelief.

It must have been a beautiful building once, but now the hotel sign lurched sideways, tiles slipped down the roof, and a tree grew out of one chimney. What a dump!

Should she make a run for her family home, which was only an hour's drive from Blackpool? It would be lovely to spend a couple of weeks on the farm. She could work on her television programme ideas there, and she knew that her mother would be delighted to hear that her only daughter was coming to stay. She'd start cooking Cherry's favourite steamed pudding the moment she heard the news.

A picture, as clear and detailed as an advertisement in a cookery magazine, popped into Cherry's mind. She could see the old cream Aga that was the centre of the farmhouse kitchen. On it sat a battered but shiny saucepan, just the right size to take a suet-crust pudding. The saucepan bubbled, the smell of cinnamon filled the air, and she knew that a Sussex Pond pudding, done her mother's way — with apples packed around the lemon so that the fruit melted into a buttery brown sugar sauce — was being prepared for her return.

'And that's half your trouble,' she told herself gloomily.

She had two choices. Go home and be spoiled for two weeks, then return to work plumper than ever with her career problems still unsolved; or step into this dingy boarding house and attempt to change her life.

She hadn't seen her mum for ages. She wanted to see her dad and the boys; maybe the weather would allow her to sit in the garden with Shep, who was now too old to herd sheep but still loved to spend time with the family. She ached with sudden homesickness.

But she wanted a date with Alan Jenkins even more. This was the first time in over three years that he'd shown even a flicker of interest in her as a woman. Would he still want to take her to dinner if she didn't lose weight?

'Don't be naive, Cherry,' she told herself, starting the engine of her car.

Because of the one-way road system, she had to drive some way down the promenade before she could turn around and drive back to the hotel. At least the hotel looked directly over

Blackpool's famous golden mile. The beach looked attractive today. Huge white clouds banked on the horizon, but the sun was out and Cherry could see the brightly-coloured parachutes of kitesurfers dipping and wheeling over the sea. Her good mood evaporated as she pulled up outside the hotel.

'Selfish beast!' she ejaculated.

Only a few minutes ago, there had been two empty parking spaces on the flat space outside the hotel. Now, however, an enormous green sports car was jauntily parked across both of the spaces, leaving no room for Cherry's little compact; and of course, double yellow lines stretched as far as the eye could see along the road.

Cherry checked for traffic wardens in both directions before leaving her car in the street. It looked clear, but she sprinted into the hotel, knowing how easy it was to get a parking ticket. Gulls screamed above her head, and in spite of her irritation she felt the sudden happiness that comes from being by the sea.

The reception area looked shabby, but every mirror sparkled, and it was as clean as a top hotel's. The scent of roses drifted from the bouquet of fresh flowers that graced a gleaming wooden desk. A slim, classy blonde in a red twin-set stood behind it. She was turning to a rank of old-fashioned wooden pigeon holes, running a finger along the gleaming brass numbers. Finding the one she wanted, she took out a key and a wodge of paper slips.

'There are a number of messages for you, Mr Cameron,' she said briskly, turning back to the bear-like figure that was standing in front of the desk, surrounded by suitcases and electronic equipment. 'Most of them are from your partner. He says that you have turned off your phone.'

'I'm supposed to be on holiday,' the man said in a deep growly voice.

The slim blonde laughed as if she found him truly funny, and the man began to say something else.

Cherry thought of traffic wardens.

'Excuse me,' she broke in. 'I can't park because there's a beast of a car in the way.'

'Just a minute, please,' snapped the blonde, gesturing that the man was first in the queue.

She needs to work on her customer relations skills! Cherry thought, feeling taken aback at her sharp dismissal, but the large figure turned to face Cherry at once. He looked like a werewolf clad in a pair of baggy trousers and a tweed jacket.

'No, no. I can wait. This lady seems to have a problem. It must be a serious problem,' he added, taking a closer look at her face with intelligent brown eyes. He had the air of being both deeply interested in her and willing to chat all day. 'You look excessively stressed. Stress is bad for your health, did you know that?'

'Parking tickets are bad for my wallet,' snapped Cherry. 'Did you know that?'

'Annoying things, aren't they,' he agreed with a wide grin.

Cherry had never seen such a shambles of a man. On closer inspection he looked more like a mad professor than a horror-movie monster. His clothes were wrinkled and unmatched. His hair hadn't been cut in months. He was taller than her. He wasn't fat, exactly, but his general shape reminded her of a teddy bear. He had an attractive grin, though, she had to admit that. It was carefree and boyish, and revealed crinkles at the sides of his eyes.

'Very annoying!' she agreed. 'That's why I'd like you to move your car.'

'My car?' he echoed, looking puzzled.

Was he having her on? Whose else could it be? Cherry fizzed with her desire to get her car off the street before she incurred a fine.

'Did you drive here?' she snapped.

'Yes.'

'Is your car green? Long? Large?'

'Sounds like my pride and joy.'

'Then move it, please! You are taking

up two parking spaces and I can't get my car off the double yellow lines outside.'

He threw back his head and laughed.

'I'm sorry,' he said. 'I didn't realise. I'm not used to the size of my new car. I'll move it at once.'

Still chuckling, he thrust a hand into one of his his baggy jacket pockets. The keys weren't there, so he fished in a few more before finally finding them in the back pocket of his trousers. He jingled them triumphantly and bounded down the steps.

A few seconds later, Cherry heard a bubbling, throaty roar as a powerful sports engine sprang into life. She walked through the double hotel doors. The long, low sports car roared forward. Gears crashed. It roared backward. There was a crunching noise from the gearbox, and it roared forward again. Cherry had never seen such an expensive car driven so badly, but there were no traffic wardens in sight, so she was able to relax and watch the comedy show calmly, feeling amused while the mad Mr Cameron re-parked his car inside the white lines.

When he had eventually managed the task, she slipped into her driving seat and drove neatly into the space that he'd created.

'You park better than I do,' he said, in his low, growly voice.

Cherry was surprised by the good humour that shone from his face. Most men were touchy about their driving skills.

'Small cars are easier to manoeuvre,' she told him.

'You are so right! I used to drive a small automatic. I only picked up this beauty this morning, and I'm not used to gears. Oh, please, let me carry your bags.'

Back in reception the slim brisk blonde was dealing with another client, an older lady with white hair who walked with the aid of a stick. Mr Cameron dropped Cherry's suitcase, turned to her and stuck out a hand.

'I'm Edward Cameron,' he said. 'It's jolly nice to meet you.'

'I'm Cherry Hawthorn.'

His handshake was pleasant. It was warm and friendly; like the man himself, she reflected.

He was examining her now in a thorough way she wasn't used to. She generally shied away from men, and they retaliated by glancing at her hunched, defensive figure, and then away. She hated men looking at her, but that was because of her own insecurity. This man was looking at her face, her neck, her torso, her legs, her feet, and then all the way back up, soaking in every detail. His attention returned to her face. The admiring expression in his eyes was frank and open. There was nothing unpleasant about this man's boyish charm and frank approval, and a tiny warm glow at the back of her brain suggested that she rather enjoyed being liked.

'I didn't expect to meet such a beautiful woman here,' he told her. 'I didn't even want to come, but now I think I'm going to enjoy myself.'

She couldn't help being amused by his frankness, but before she could ask him why he'd come to the spa if he didn't want to, the slim blonde called him to the reception desk.

'If you could just sign here, Mr Cameron, then I'll show you your room.'

Edward Cameron paused at the bottom of the hotel stairs and gave Cherry a gigantic wave. 'See you at dinner,' he cried.

To her great surprise, her arm lifted and she waved back, but she stopped herself replying aloud. Even if she'd fancied a dalliance with an eccentric hairy bear of a man, which she didn't, there was her promise to Alan to consider and their date at the smart restaurant to look forward to.

How odd life was. She'd gone years without a man even looking at her . . . now, not only was she promised to the most desirable man at the television studios, but the very next man she met seemed to like her too. Odd, but rather nice!

Her bedroom was shabby, but it was spotless, and the linen was new and luxurious. The old hotel must have been grand once. Her room was spacious, and it had French windows that opened onto a balcony, which in turn overlooked the sea. Cherry rushed to fling open the windows. A sea breeze blew in, fluttering the curtains and tugging at her skirt. There must be a million seagulls in this town, she thought, listening to the row overhead. She knew the white birds could be a nuisance, but they did look pretty, flying and tumbling in the blue sky. She could smell salt, and way off in the distance she could hear the electrifying thump of fairground music.

Cherry felt happy as she showered and got changed to go downstairs, more alive than she had in a long time. Holiday excitement pulsed though her veins and she was suddenly glad that she'd come. Not only did she have a whole two weeks' vacation, but she was starting an exciting new chapter of her life — one that would begin with a date in Manchester's trendiest venue with none other than Alan Jenkins! Could life get any better?

Cherry walked confidently downstairs, but then hesitated by the doorway of the hotel bar. To distract her nerves, she looked over the decor of the dark cave of the interior of the bar. It was the same mixture of styles that she was beginning to expect. The carpet, walls and furniture had clearly seen better days, but the room was spotless. The bar brass glittered, the glasses shone, and a dramatic flower arrangement graced the polished wood of the bar.

'Cherry! Over here!' bellowed a loud voice. 'I saved you a seat.'

The madly waving figure was perched on a barstool like a bear in a circus, but Cherry was so glad to see someone she knew that she forgot that she'd decided not to encourage him. She walked straight over and climbed onto the stool. Edward instantly called for a drink.

The cocktails were non-alcoholic and low calorie, but they looked pretty. Cherry picked a green concoction that tinkled with ice and was garnished with mint leaves. The first sip made her screw up her face.

'Oh! That's bitter!'

'Sugar's bad for you,' Edward replied. 'It's the most unnatural substance. Our bodies evolved to eat berries, with maybe the occasional lick of honey, but now we cram them with refined chemicals . . . oh, I'm giving you too much information.' He broke off and gazed at her with mournful brown eyes. 'Harold says people find too many facts boring. He says that when I start dating, I must never, never bore my date by shoving too many facts at them. And what do I do? The very first chance I get, I lecture you. I'm sorry.'

He looked so heartbroken that

Cherry had to comfort him.

'I thought it was interesting.'

His brown eyes lit up, and if he'd had a tail, it would have been wagging.

His expression made it so clear that he was interested in her that Cherry added hastily: 'We're not dating so it doesn't matter what you say.'

The light in his eyes dimmed, but then he looked hopeful.

'We could be friends, though, couldn't we?'

Warmth and friendliness poured from the man. Although it was June, his open hearty largeness made Cherry think of Christmas. She could imagine this man in his element by a roaring fire, laughing and handing out presents.

'We could be friends,' she said, with firm emphasis on the last word. She had no intention of leading him on. 'There's an important man waiting for the new me.'

The disappointment in his brown eyes was flatteringly clear.

'What's wrong with the old you?' he

asked, looking as if he really wanted to know. 'I think you're stunning.'

Flattery it might be, but his words still made her glow. For a split second she felt happy in her own skin, then she remembered that the television company considered her too ugly to represent them in public. She thought of Alan telling her to lose weight and get some exercise.

'Isn't it obvious?' Cherry replied.

He looked puzzled and uncertain, as if he wasn't sure how to respond to her. She took another slug of her drink.

'Ugh! It's as sour as a lemon!'

Edward brightened, glanced around and whispered like a conspirator into her ear.

'Would you like some sugar?'

There was no way she could finish her drink as it was.

'You have sugar? Oh, yes, please!'

He hadn't changed for dinner. He was still in the tweed jacket. Cherry watched him fishing in the baggy pockets and wondered what else he had hidden in their depths. He finally unearthed two small packets bearing the logo of a motorway service station, and emptied one into each drink, stirring them so vigorously with the cocktail swizzle stick that mint leaves swirled and ice clattered and leapt out of the glasses and skittered along the bar.

'Oops!' he said, grinning. 'We'll get caught.'

Cherry couldn't help grinning back. 'Nobody noticed,' she whispered.

His eyes were warm with fun. They were like two kids with a big secret.

'Cheers!' he said, holding out his glass.

'Cheers!' Cherry replied, her glass clinking against his.

The drink was a whole lot sweeter-tasting with sugar in it, but as soon as she'd downed it, Cherry felt guilty. She wasn't a child any more. She was an adult and she'd come here with a specific goal in mind, one that she'd never achieve if she snuck around breaking the rules.

'Another drink?' Edward asked. 'I have a couple more packets somewhere. He began patting his bulging pockets, looking for the forbidden sweetener. Those pockets were big enough to hide a whole sugar refinery never mind a few sticks. *He's probably got two weeks' worth of forbidden calories hidden in there*, thought Cherry.

'No thank you,' she snapped. 'And if you're going to break the rules, I think I'll stay away from you.'

She slid off her stool. The bar had filled while they'd been chatting. People of all sizes clustered around the tables or stood in groups. She could hear people saying things like, 'I'm from the Midlands,' and 'I work in a bank', the kind of chatter that helps people who don't know one another make connections. Which group should she join?

And then she felt a hand on her arm. Edward turned her to face him.

'Cherry, I know why you are mad. I shouldn't have tempted you.'

'No, you shouldn't!' she replied, still feeling grumpy.

His face was calm and smiling, but she was suddenly aware of the man's strength of character as he spoke firmly.

'I didn't make you take that sugar. Don't blame me for your lapse.'

His brown eyes were open, honest, kind, understanding, and he was right. The anger she'd felt at herself had lashed out at him.

'Don't tempt me again,' she told him. 'I'm like Oscar Wilde. I can resist anything but temptation.'

Edward laughed.

'That's very clever,' he approved. 'Is Oscar Wilde staying at the spa?'

Here was a man who looked like a professor, with intelligence beaming out of every cell of his body, who had never heard of Oscar Wilde! Cherry was astonished.

'He's a famous author,' she told him.

'I've never had time to read any literature. It's one of the things I'm going to do now my work is finished.'

He looked at her hopefully. 'Maybe you could help me by suggesting some titles?'

A reverberating metal boom startled them both. They turned to look at the source of the noise.

'Oh, a real old-fashioned gong,' Edward said, beaming with pleasure.

The brisk blonde was standing at the end of the bar. 'Ladies and gentlemen. Dinner is ready. Would you please make your way to the dining room?'

And she gestured with the gong stick at a doorway that led into a dining room. All the people in the bar began trouping into the dining room. Although the wallpaper was peeling, it was no surprise to see brand-new white table cloths and fresh flowers on every table.

Bumbling and clumsy Edward might be, but as she sat down, Cherry suspected that it was no accident he'd found them a table for two in one corner. A man had never made the effort to get her alone before. She wasn't the kind of woman that men fought to sit by. His interest made her feel warm and happy inside. People flowed into the room like locusts, swarming over every chair and filling all the tables. Chairs scraped and chatter rose. Cherry did a rapid headcount, and then realised that her companion was also counting. He finished first.

'I make it seventeen,' Edward said, 'including us, of course.'

'I got it to eighteen,' Cherry argued.

'It's seventeen. I'm never wrong about numbers.'

Before Cherry had finished her recount, the missing guest who brought the group total up to eighteen appeared in the doorway, and a sudden silence fell.

She was a curvy little redhead with very unusual clear turquoise eyes, and she wore nothing but sparkle and green feathers. She teetered into the room on glittery high-heels, then stopped and looked around her at the full restaurant. The other guests were a distinctly ordinary group. Cherry, who'd chosen a black frock with short sleeves, was among the more formally dressed. Most people were casual in caftans or slacks and T-shirts.

The redhead blinked her long false lashes and revolved slowly around the room, displaying a green tail made of green feathers and a great deal of bare skin. She was dressed for a Brazilian carnival. Her bikini was made of three miniscule sequined flowers, and the emerald feathers in her headdress matched those on her peacock of a tail.

A shrill wolf-whistle rent the air.

'You can come and sit on my knee, darling!' invited a man with a lecherous voice. He had a red face and a golf-shirt in the most revolting shade of yellow, which strained over a pot belly.

'Behave yourself, Stanley!' snapped the female sitting next to him. She was wearing the kind of white outfit that is meant to show off a tan, but the harsh white only emphasised the fact that her skin was the colour of orange leather.

She glared at the redhead.

Laughter rose all around them. The redhead peered this way and that around the room. She was looking for an empty chair, Cherry realised, and there didn't seem to be one. She saw the girl's bottom lip shake and felt instant sympathy for her. Cherry leapt to her feet and looked around her for a chair, a waiter or the brisk blonde, anyone to help her. Then Edward got up so quickly that he knocked his chair over. He crossed the room, tapped the redhead on the shoulder and gestured towards Cherry.

'I'm Edward. Please, come and sit with me and Cherry.'

'Thanks,' said the redhead.

She turned her turquoise gaze towards him, melting if he were a knight in shining armour.

A waiter appeared, a chair was brought, another set of silver knives and forks were squeezed onto the white cloth, and the redhead quickly sat down. Close up, Cherry could see that the girl was wearing a thick tan body stocking. The sexy, glittery bikini was sewn on top. She was showing no bare skin at all, but from a distance, and worn over the girl's ample curves, the effect had been dynamite.

Edward examined the girl with frank interest and Cherry felt a tug of jealousy. Don't be a dog-in-the-manger, she scolded herself furiously. You are taken; you've already turned him down. It would be nice for him to meet someone else.

But she was glad to see that the look in his brown eyes as he gazed at the little redhead was different from the way he'd looked at her. There was no warm admiration, no appreciation of her sexiness. He looked more like a supportive big brother.

The little redhead sniffed back a tear and looked at Cherry.

'I hope you don't mind me sitting with youse.'

'It's nice to have your company. I'm Cherry Hawthorn, and this is Edward Cameron.'

The redhead sniffed again.

'Me name's Angelina. I'm from Liverpool, and I wish I'd never come. Those people were laughing at me, weren't they?'

'No they weren't. Take no notice of them,' Cherry soothed, the social white lie rising automatically to her lips.

But at the same moment, Edward said, 'Yes, they were laughing at you.'

Angelina looked at Edward. Her turquoise eyes were shiny with tears.

'Is it me clothes? I'm dressed all wrong, aren't I?'

'I think you look lovely,' Cherry told her, with perfect truth. She could feel Edward's sceptical gaze on her face. Feeling goaded into being more truthful, she added, 'I think people were surprised by your carnival outfit, that's all.'

Angelina sniffed a third time.

'Is this get-up wrong for dinner at this place? I thought you had to get poshed up, like, and they told me at work this dress would be perfect because Blackpool's famous for dancing and the spa made a point of it.'

Edward beamed at her.

'Your dress is fantastic, but it's for doing the samba in, not for eating dinner. I read a very interesting paper the other day about dress and social codes. As a species, we like people to fit in. We have a very low tolerance for the wrong outfit when it's worn at the wrong time.'

He broke off and gazed at the incomprehension on Angelina's little face.

'Sorry,' he grinned. 'I'm spouting too much information again. It's a bad habit of mine.'

Angelina's expression warmed into a smile.

'These feathers are a proper pain. I'm glad I don't have to wear them.'

She took off the elaborate headdress and laid it on the floor beside her in a feathery heap. A quick wriggle of the curvy bottom, and the emerald tail followed suit. It was none of her business, of course, but Cherry was glad to see that Edward paid no attention to the wriggle.

One tiny ting of a fork tinkling on a glass made utter silence fall. The brisk blonde, wearing a red shift dress that made her look like Jackie Kennedy, introduced herself as Poppy and continued to speak to them all.

'Starting this evening, and continuing tomorrow, I'd like to meet with you all individually. You will find a schedule of private appointments on the board in reception for your medical checks and your makeover sessions. It is a beautiful evening, so I strongly suggest that you try a walk on our beautiful promenade after supper.'

She gestured to the slim, very fit man who stood next to her.

'Step forward, Ryan. Everyone, meet your personal fitness trainer, Ryan. Over the next few days, he will help you work out the programme that best suits your body, and over the next two weeks he'll help you stick with it.'

A few nervous laughs spluttered around the room as Ryan bounced forward and gave them all a cheery wave. He didn't have regular features, but as you might expect, he appeared to be handsome because of his perfectly toned body.

He'll have his work cut out with us, Cherry thought. She loathed all forms of exercise, and most of the people in the room looked as if they agreed with her.

'Step forward, Serena!' cried Poppy.

One of the most striking features about the lithe blonde who shimmied forward was the very calm expression in her wide blue eyes. Her waterfall of fine, natural blonde hair, stunning though it was, seemed of secondary importance. It was no surprise when Poppy introduced her as the yoga teacher and recommended that everyone join the morning session, which was held in the ballroom.

'Or on the roof, if the weather is warm enough,' Serena added.

A hum of conversation rose and several people reached for their knives and forks, thinking that the introduction was over and they could eat, but Poppy tapped her silver fork on the glass again. Instant silence fell and every face turned to watch her. Some people have natural authority, Cherry mused. This woman was so full of it she could boss an army.

'I need to say a word about the food before we serve dinner. You'll find that the cuisine is healthy and nutritious, and please, do eat as much as you like, we are not about dieting here, but your food may taste different to what you are used to. We use very little oil and, perhaps the biggest challenge for most of you, hardly any sugar.'

Cherry glanced at Edward when sugar was mentioned. He'd turned his head to look at her. His brown eyes met her hazel gaze, and they smiled ruefully at the same instant, drawn together by their secret misdemeanour, before turning back to listen to Poppy.

'You may find your food and drink unpalatable for a couple of days. I would ask you to stick with it, please. Your taste buds will adapt and I can promise you that by the end of the two weeks you won't want to go back to heavily sweetened food. Now, please enjoy your meal.'

The food did taste good, although it featured rather more in the way of vegetables than Cherry would normally select, but she wasn't so sure about the lack of sugar.

'How do you drink your tea and coffee?' she asked Edward.

'Milk and three sugars,' he admitted. 'How do you drink yours?'

'Cream and two sugars,' she sighed. 'What about you, Angelina?'

'I have milk and sugar, and a cigarette as well. I suppose I'll have to go outside after me dinner,' Angelina said, poking at her food. 'What's this curly thing like a black slug on me plate, do you know?'

'It's a slice of baked aubergine,' Cherry said.

Angelina nibbled one corner.

'Oh, it tastes all right, it just looked funny. What did that woman mean about not dieting? I've come here to go on a diet.'

'Me too,' Cherry said.

Angelina's round turquoise eyes opened wide.

'You don't need to diet,' she protested.

'You mustn't change a thing!' Edward insisted.

Angelina continued, 'I thought you'd come here for the relaxing, like, you know, the spa and the yoga and all that.' The expression in her eyes was genuine and wistful as she gazed at Cherry. 'You don't need no makeover, neither. That dress you've got on is lovely. I've got no dress sense, me. I can't wait for my makeover. And after tonight, I'm never asking those cats in the office what to wear. I felt proper stupid.'

'Never mind,' Edward pointed out cheerfully. 'It led to you sitting down at our table and talking to us, in this universe, that is. Some people think that there is an infinite number of universes, and everything that could possibly have happened in our past, but did not, did actually occur in some other universe. When you think about it, that means there could be millions of worlds where things worked out slightly differently. For example, we three might have come to the same spa, but ended up never actually sitting together — '

He broke off and grimaced.

'Whoops! Sorry.'

Cherry had to chuckle at Angelina's expression. She was regarding Edward with a mixture of awe and confusion on her transparent little face.

'Are you a professor?' she asked him.

His grin was cheerful.

'No, I've never been to university, although it's one of the things that I might do now that my work is finished.'

It was an odd way of talking about a career. Cherry had never heard of anyone finishing work and then getting qualified! She leaned forward to ask him what he meant, but Angelina got in first.

'What do you do?'

'I'm a kind of mathematician.'

She beamed.

'I'm an accountant. I just passed me final exams.'

'And this holiday is your reward?'

'Yes, but I couldn't have come if I hadn't won some money on the lottery.'

'I can't believe that! You work with numbers and you still play the lottery!'

'I only do it to join in at work. And we won!'

Edward shook his head.

'People don't understand that the odds against them are astronomical.'

'I'm part of a work syndicate myself,' Cherry told them both. 'I do know how unlikely a win is, but suppose the group hit the jackpot and I wasn't a part of it? I'd be the only person in the office on Monday morning!'

They all laughed, and Cherry realised that she was enjoying herself.

Edward smiled and said, 'My mother

insists on buying a ticket every week. I wrote a computer programme to see how long it would take her lucky numbers to come up. It's been running for ninety-seven thousand years so far.'

'And she still plays?'

'Oh, yes. I'm still three-year-old Teddy in her mind, and who takes advice from a toddler?'

They all laughed again.

'I like the name Teddy. It suits you better than Edward,' Cherry said, thinking what a big cuddly bear of a man he was.

'I agree,' Angelina said, beaming.

Teddy grinned cheerfully and spoke to Cherry.

'I like the name Teddy, if you do!'

Angelina grinned wickedly.

'Knock knock!'

'Who's there?' Teddy responded obediently.

'Teddy.'

'Teddy who?'

'Teddy is the first day of the rest of your life.'

It was silly, but the old chestnut sent them into gales of laughter.

Cherry felt that sudden rush of happiness again. She hadn't expected to enjoy herself at the spa, but here she was, laughing and chatting. Because she worked so hard, she very rarely socialised, now she relished the feeling of being out with friends. It would be like this when she went for her promised meal with Alan, only better. The thought of Alan reminded her that she wasn't at the spa to enjoy herself, but to make serious changes to her life. She got to her feet.

'It was very nice to meet you both. I have the first appointment with Poppy in the morning, which means getting up early, so I'll say goodnight.'

Teddy stood up.

'I'm sorry you're leaving us so early,' he said, his low growly voice sounding forlorn.

'I'll see you tomorrow,' Cherry pointed out, thinking how sweet he was.

Perhaps her warm feelings had

shown. His brown eyes lit up like Christmas tree decorations and he beamed hugely.

'Great!'

She was totally unprepared for his reaction, or hers. Her heart thumped. Why, he seemed to genuinely like her! The thought thrilled her and scared her at the same time.

3

Breakfast was interesting rather than delicious. It was big on brown bread and sugar-free cereals, small on all Cherry's favourites such as butter, cream and milk. There was plenty to eat: you could even have a cooked breakfast of poached eggs and mush-rooms and grilled tomatoes, but somehow she couldn't fancy toast without butter. And coffee without milk and sugar was just wrong. After one bitter mouthful she pushed aside her cup and left the contents undrunk. Apple juice, unsweetened of course, was not at all successful in waking her up, and she felt distinctly grumpy as she went for her appointment with Poppy.

Gold spectacles covered Poppy's light-blue eyes this morning and she wore a white coat over another red dress. She was exceedingly thorough as she weighed and measured Cherry, and then took her medical history in a businesslike way. She had quite a few medical gadgets that Cherry had never even seen before, and she used them all with relish, filling in the blanks on a long, long chart. The last measurement she took was blood pressure, then she keyed all the results into a computer programme before turning to Cherry with a decisive air.

'Very healthy, I'm glad to say. You could perhaps do with shedding a couple of pounds, but a few simple lifestyle changes will take care of that.'

'I need to lose more than a few pounds!' Cherry protested. 'Don't you mean a few stone?'

Poppy's blue eyes blazed over the top of her spectacles.

'I do not!'

'But I must lose weight! That's what I've come here for.'

'Come over here and look at this chart, Cherry. Here is your height, your

60

age, your body-fat index, and here is the acceptable maximum and minimum weight for your particular situation. These are government figures, and, as medical thinking stands now, anyone within this range is healthy. You are here, a couple of pounds over the top line. I would not encourage you to diet.'

Cherry was dumbfounded.

'But, but I'm too fat!' she mumbled. 'I always have been. You don't know what it's like being me.'

Poppy's blue eyes were not exactly sympathetic, but they were understanding.

'Have you been on many diets?'

'No, no. It wasn't possible at home, and then it seemed too late to bother. I was set in my ways.' Cherry opened her hands wide in a helpless gesture. 'I like to cook and eat, and I was busy with my career.'

'That's excellent news. I don't approve of diets. What kind of food do you eat, and why?'

'I grew up on a farm, and I still eat

the same kind of food — hearty and home grown. My mum taught me to cook. She isn't happy unless she is cooking and we are eating. The men need the calories, of course, but I don't like physical labour, so I've always been this size, or bigger.'

'There's nothing wrong with your size. You may not be a stick-thin model, but you are normal.'

Poppy got to her feet and drew Cherry to the end of her office, then gestured at a wall chart that ran like a border across the complete wall. It was a kind of diagram with a long line of female figures running across it.

'I call this the wall of truth,' Poppy said. 'Have you seen a diagram like this on reality television shows?'

'I don't think so.'

'Well, as you can see, the lifesize female figures start at this end of the wall, very, very thin, and get bigger by increments reaching seriously over-weight at the other end. All I want you to do is to look at the outlines of the figures and decide where you fit on the chart. What size are you, Cherry?'

'Not the largest, which is a relief, but otherwise I don't know.'

'Make your best guess,' Poppy said, and there was no disobeying her.

'Here,' Cherry admitted, picking a podgy figure on the spectrum. She cheated a little. Knowing Poppy didn't think she was fat, Cherry picked a figure several sizes smaller than her real size.

Poppy shook her head.

'Here,' she said, indicating a curvy figure three sizes smaller again.

'No!'

'Truly! That's you, Cherry, as other people see you, not as you see yourself.'

Poppy whipped out a tape measure to prove her point, but Cherry still couldn't believe it.

'That can't be right. I was teased at school — '

'Oh, Cherry, everyone's teased at school. You don't have to let it affect your whole life.'

63

Cherry didn't want to tell anyone how dreadful the teasing had made her feel, and she had another argument to use.

'I do when it affects my career. I'm not the only one who thinks I'm overweight!'

'What are you talking about?'

Cherry explained how her company had refused to allow her to represent them in public, and why. There was a furious look in Poppy's blue eyes.

'I never heard such nonsense! This boss of yours, Alan, is he playing some kind of game with you?'

'No, no, I'm sure he's not.'

'It smells extremely fishy to me. I can't think why you didn't speak with your Human Resources department. You might want to consult an employment lawyer. Most companies crumble when you point out that they are discriminating against you and that you'll fight them in court. I'm prepared to write you a letter stating that your weight is well within the accepted range of normality.'

Cherry felt as if she'd sat on a firecracker. Poppy had shaken her up and showed Cherry what her proper course of action should have been. What a wimpy fool she'd been to cave in without a fight.

'I should have insisted on a meeting with personnel. It was stupid of me. I didn't think. Thank you so much for your advice, I'm going to take it! I'll get a lawyer, and a doctor's letter and do everything properly.'

Poppy's blue eyes peered over the top of the gold spectacles once more.

'I am a doctor,' she sighed. 'Didn't you read the information in the lobby?'

The world spun around Cherry and she suddenly recognised Poppy's brisk manner and slightly bossy way of speaking as being typical of a busy doctor.

'I'm sorry. I haven't had time to look at the brochures yet.'

Cherry got up to leave, thinking their interview was over, but she was crisply motioned to stay and the pale blue eyes regarded her steadily over the tops of the gold-rimmed reading spectacles.

'Well, I am a doctor, a proper one, and it behoves you to take my advice. Your weight is fine, although we may need to talk more about the issues surrounding your self-esteem and body image, but what I urgently need to discuss with you this morning is the appallingly low level of your fitness!'

Cherry felt utterly crushed by the time Poppy had finished lecturing her. She was then packed off to see Ryan in the gym area. He echoed Poppy's every word, but at least he did so with tact. He laughed when Cherry confessed what a telling off she'd had.

'You'll get the truth from Doctor Poppy,' he pointed out. 'And you'll get the very best advice, which isn't always the case in politer health spas. Now, can you touch your toes? Don't worry. Just give me the best you can do . . . I see. You walk from the couch to the fridge and that's about it, right?'

'I'm afraid so. Poppy said that my blood-pressure is too high, so I have to exercise more,' Cherry told Ryan. 'And I know she's right. I'm awkward though, and stiff. I hate exercise, I always have.'

'The trick is to find something you enjoy.'

'There is not one single form of exercise on this planet that I can ever imagine enjoying!'

'There'll be something,' Ryan told her firmly. 'Even if we have to try every activity going to find the one you'll love. Do you swim? No? Never mind. Come along with me and have a splash in the shallow end. I'll teach you a few strokes, and you can reward yourself with a relax in the sauna afterwards.'

The pool looked like a set for a luxury movie. Sunlight streamed through glass panels in ceiling and sparkled on the blue water. It was deliciously warm, and full of green plants.

Ryan looked proud of his domain.

'Unlike the rest of the sports area, which needs a total refurbishment, we only had to give the pool a deep clean. Isn't it gorgeous?'

'Heavenly,' Cherry said truthfully. 'It's a comfort to know that I'm going to drown in such a beautiful environment.'

She didn't make much progress when it came to swimming, but she did spend a pleasant morning. Physically it was very calming to don a white towelling robe and relax on a lounger, mentally she was thinking furiously. Doctor Poppy had given her a lot to reflect upon.

At lunch time, Teddy gave her his usual huge wave.

'Over here!' he boomed.

She couldn't help being warmed by his enthusiasm, and she felt safe in joining him, because there was a chaperone sitting next to him, a jolly-looking lady with white hair, who was introduced to her as Sukie.

'Come and join us, my dear. Teddy

was telling me all about his work. It sounds most interesting, dear, although surely you missed out on a lot while you were concentrating on your studies? I hope your work will prove to be worth the sacrifices you've made. It certainly sounds as if it will be.'

A flush reddened his cheeks, and he looked pleased. Then he frowned.

'I feel odd now it's finished. There's a hole in my life. I don't know what to do with myself.'

'Get married and have a family, dear.'

Teddy beamed.

'That's exactly what my business partner, Harold, says. He says that I must start dating, and he's sent me here for a makeover. He says I've got no social skills, and that no woman would look at a scruffy hulk like me!'

Sukie looked him over with the air of a wise and grandmotherly owl.

'Any woman would be glad to meet a man like you,' she advised him. 'New clothes and a haircut wouldn't hurt, dear, but it's what's inside a man that matters.' Then she gave a rich chuckle. 'Money and success don't hurt, either. I don't think you'll have any difficulty finding a nice woman.'

Teddy glanced at Cherry.

'I've already met one, but she's taken.'

His eyes were so sad that she felt the urge to comfort him, but what could she say? He seemed like a lovely man, but he wasn't a hero to her the way Alan Jenkins was. Why, she'd been in love with Alan for three years. A thrill went down her spine as she remembered that there were only fifteen days until her date with him at the Correspondent's Club!

Sukie got up, moving slowly and awkwardly.

'Time for my appointment with Poppy,' she said.

'Good luck,' Cherry sent after her with feeling.

A man in a shiny cat-sick-yellow golf shirt, who'd been sitting alone at the next table, lounged over to join them.

'What the dickens is that old biddy doing here?' he asked scornfully, gazing after Sukie. 'It's a bit late for her to start bothering what she looks like. Perhaps she wants to be a beautiful corpse.'

He laughed at his own joke. His laugh was horrible. He really did go 'yuk, yuk, yuk', like a character in a comic-book.

Teddy gazed scornfully at the laughing man.

'Sukie is only seventy-five,' he said coolly. 'She could easily have thirty or more years to live. Why shouldn't she take care of her health?'

The golf-shirted man gawped in shock. He opened his mouth to reply, but Cherry would never know what he would have said. Teddy, warming to his subject, carried on speaking with enthusiasm.

'There was a fascinating piece in the New Scientist last week by an American gerontologist, I forget his exact name, Doctor Chang Woo Lin, I think, but anyway, he says that the children who are being born today could easily live to be one hundred and fifty years or more because of the advances in medical science.'

The golf-shirted man stuck out a hand to stop him.

'Yeah, very interesting, mate,' he said, his tone making it clear he meant the exact opposite. He walked back to his table and sat down alone, looking deeply offended.

Teddy turned to Cherry.

'I'm sorry! I was lecturing again. I forget other people don't find these matters interesting. Cherry, what's the matter? Are you angry with me? Oh, you're laughing! But I wasn't trying to be funny.'

'Teddy, you are priceless.'

'I'm hopeless socially,' he muttered, and there was a despondent droop to his shoulders that went to her heart. Cherry put a hand on his arm.

'We don't want to socialise with that horrible man. He's the one who started cat-calling at Angelina last night. You get on with her all right, and me, and Sukie.'

Teddy looked down at her, an eager light in his eyes.

'You mean it's not my fault? That nice people are easy to talk to?'

Cherry thought it over.

'To a great extent,' she told him. 'But sometimes people take a while to get to know one another, so it's not a hard and fast rule.'

'People are much more difficult to deal with than figures,' Teddy told her, with the air of a man reporting a grave discovery.

'You talk as if you've never dealt with people before,' Cherry, said, feeling curious.

'I haven't, apart from Harold. I worked on my own at home, you see.'

'What about when you were a child?'

'I grew up in the country, in Cumbria. Nobody lived near our farm. I took the bus to school, but it was a complete waste of my time.'

'I hated school, too,' Cherry said, 'and I grew up on a farm, so we have lots in common. I was teased all the time. Why didn't you like school?'

'Because I wanted to study,' was the surprising reply.

Cherry lifted her eyebrows.

'Isn't that what school is for? My school made us study too hard! You'll have to explain what you mean.'

'I loved mathematics, and engineering, and all we did in class was baby numbers.' He looked at Cherry earnestly, as if willing her to understand. 'Imagine if you wanted to read interesting books, like those written by that amusing author you were telling me about, Oscar Wilde, and all people would give you was one page with 'SEE SPOT RUN' written on it, and made you look at it for hours!'

'A child genius,' diagnosed Cherry.

'I don't know about that, but I loved maths. I read everything I could find, but there wasn't much, even when I went to secondary school and could use the library. The Internet saved me.'

His face lit with remembered happiness and Cherry understood how much the discovery had meant to him.

'I could get my hands on academic papers, engineering texts, even use email to talk to the people who were full of interesting ideas and they took my work seriously. It was fantastic!'

'Is that how you met your business partner?'

'Harold? No, he lives near me and we went to primary school together. When we were eleven, I went to the local school in Newcastle, but his parents sent him to boarding school. We used to play together in the holidays though, and we kept in touch.'

Teddy grinned at Cherry.

'You'll meet him tonight. He's coming to check on me!'

'He sounds like a good friend.'

'The best,' Teddy said simply. 'He's always taken care of all the boring stuff so I was free to work.'

At last, thought Cherry!

'I've been wanting to know about your mystery career. Please will you explain it to me?'

Unfortunately, she couldn't understand the explanation! He tried to tell her what he did all the way through lunch, but eventually she pushed aside her undrunk cup of tea and laughed up at him.

'I think I'd need a five-year course of math and physics before I could grasp what you have been doing and I still don't understand why you've had to give up!'

'I've not given up, I've finished,' Teddy said earnestly. 'My main work is complete.'

'What happens next?'

'I don't know. Most mathematicians do their best work under thirty, and I'm thirty next year, so I may never come up with another radical theory that is completely new, but I could have fun trying! Harold wants me to spend more time on practical applications because they make so much money.'

'You're a kind of inventor,' Cherry realised. 'What kind of things do you invent? Will I have heard of any of them?'

'Not unless you work in oil or gas.'

'I'm in television,' Cherry said. 'I know a little bit about everything. Give me an example of one of your inventions.'

'The most useful was a new sealing process for sections of oil pipe. The process means that the pipes won't leak and it prevents environmental disasters, so all the companies use it now.'

'How did you get into that field?'

'It was Harold's idea. Harold shows me problems and then when I've solved them, he goes off and turns my ideas into money.'

'Does he want money for his benefit?' Cherry asked, feeling protective on Teddy's behalf. He was so much the absent-minded professor that she could imagine him being taken advantage of.

But Teddy was grinning cheerfully.

'He uses all the cash we make for his

estate's benefit. He comes from an old border family. They are all too posh to dabble in commerce, so of course his old home is more or less bankrupt, or it was until we started working together. He's doing a grand job of restoring it.'

'He's restoring his house on your money?'

'Thanks to Harold I've still got more than I could spend in three lifetimes. He'd be welcome to have every penny, if he wanted it. It's not important. I'd soon get more. Money's not hard to make. All you do is invent something and the loot pours in.'

Cherry was still mulling over that incredible statement when Teddy turned to her with a smile in his warm brown eyes.

'I'd like to ask you a favour. I know there's a special man in your life, and I'm not asking you for a date, but Angelina told me that she'd never been out to a decent restaurant in her life, which seems wrong, and I'd like to impress Harold this evening by showing him how well I'm doing with beautiful women. Would you come out with us as a foursome? There's a place in the Lake District, near Cartmel, that has two Michelin stars. I think Angelina would like it, and they specialise in healthy options, so I wouldn't be tempting you.'

Cherry accepted with pleasure. What a nice man he is, she thought, as they made arrangements to meet in reception that evening, and what an unusual one. His life story was intriguing.

'I'll look forward to it,' Teddy said, lumbering to his feet. 'What's your programme this afternoon?'

'I'm going to have a private yoga session followed by a massage. How about you?'

'The makeover for men,' Teddy said, grimacing. 'I'm sure they'll want to cut my hair.'

Cherry laughed up at him.

'I'm sure you'll look better for it!'

4

Teddy looked so much better for his haircut that Cherry didn't recognise him. She looked around the reception area that evening and thought she must be early because Teddy and Angelina were not down from their hotel rooms yet. Two handsome men in dinner jackets were standing by the flower arrangement, talking to an elegant redhead she hadn't seen before. Her auburn curls were swept up and held back with pearls, and she was wearing a classically cut dark-green dress that Cherry couldn't help admiring.

And then the larger of the two men spotted her, turned and waved vigorously. She recognised Teddy's exuberant body language, but what a transformation! He looked stylish in his well-cut tuxedo, and shorter hair suited him. He was actually good-looking under all that fuzz!

'No!' she cried in surprise. 'Is it really you?'

A flush tinged his brown cheeks and he held out both hands to her. Cherry took them without thinking, looking him up and down in disbelief.

'You clean up pretty good, Teddy.'

The smile in his brown eyes was shy.

'Thank you. Moira the makeover lady is a bit of a wizard.'

'I'm booking in with her tomorrow!'

'You don't need a makeover, Cherry,' the redhead said earnestly. 'That's another lovely frock you're wearing.'

'Angelina! I didn't recognise you, either! What an evening!'

The turquoise eyes brimmed with innocent happiness.

'I love me new green dress. I'm dressed right for dinner tonight, aren't I?'

'You look perfect!' Cherry was able to assure her with honesty.

Teddy kept hold of her hand as he

introduced her to his business partner. Harold was a tall, thin blond man who made her think of a heron or a stork: some kind of thin, slow-moving bird.

'Evening,' he said, giving her a long, slow measuring look before his grey eyes lit up in a smile.

Cherry couldn't help exclaiming again over the transformations. She delayed them all a few seconds while she examined the back of Angelina's updo, so they were still in the lobby when the man in the shiny cat-sick-yellow golf-shirt burst out of the lift. He dragged out several suitcases before sending the lift upstairs again with a fierce stab at the button. He was crimson in the face when he turned to them.

'I'm leaving this dump at once!' he snarled at them. 'And if you've got any sense, you'll do the same.'

The lift doors dinged open once more and his orange-faced wife shot out. Her violent temper was not improved by the struggle she was having with several handbags, an enormous vanity case, a travelling set of heated rollers and three suit bags with bits of evening-dress poking out. She couldn't wait to share her woes. 'That Poppy woman is the rudest person I've ever met in my life! Calls herself a doctor! Huh! I'm going to check with the Medical Council. I know her sort!'

'I'll set the television watchdogs on her,' bawled the man. 'I'll give this place such terrible reviews that no one will ever come here again and she'll be ruined.'

'What's the problem?' Teddy enquired mildly.

The man answered first.

'She told me I needed more exercise. I play golf twice a week already. I told her that was enough exercise for any man. She had the cheek to suggest that it doesn't count as exercise if you use a golf cart and then she as good as called me lazy! We're leaving, I said. I don't have to put up with being insulted.'

'And has Doctor Poppy upset you,

madam?' Teddy enquired, turning to the leather-skinned woman. His voice was mild, but they all heard the emphasis on the title 'doctor'.

'She told me I had to stop using sun-beds! Dowdy old bat! What would she know about style? I take pride in my appearance.'

'Studies have shown that excessive use of sun-beds frequently leads to . . . '

Teddy yelped and stopped mid-flow. Cherry saw Harold remove the foot he'd placed on the toe of Teddy's shoe.

The yellow-shirted man glared at them with the furious eyes of a farmyard bull.

'Blooming mad house, this is! I'm glad to be leaving. Here's our taxi! Come on, driver. Pick up those cases, chop, chop!'

Harold lifted a languid eyebrow as he watched their departing figures.

'So nice to witness openness, flexibility and willingness to change,' he drawled. 'Our table is booked for nine o'clock, so shall we make a move?'

Although they were going out as foursome, Harold's car was another two-seater, a long, low, fire-engine red roadster, so Cherry realised that she'd be alone with Teddy on the drive. He smiled at her.

'It's a gorgeous evening. Shall we drive with the top down, if I can find how to accomplish that feat?'

Harold seemed to have the same idea. The roof of the red car came apart, lifted up into the air, then tucked itself away into various recesses like folds of origami. Seconds later, Teddy must have found the right button, for the roof of the green car followed suit. Angelina clapped her hands and squealed with delight.

'That's well good,' she cried.

Harold strolled over to Teddy's car and handed Cherry a large blue silk head square. It was printed with horseshoes and bore the logo of a famous French company in one corner.

'Little tip for you, Teddy: always keep a couple of scarves in the glove compartment of a convertible for your female passengers,' he said.

'Thank you,' Cherry said, feeling very glamorous and European as she tied the luxurious scarf over her hair.

The burble of two powerful engines rent the night air and they were off. For a sickening moment Cherry wondered if the men would be able to resist racing one another in their potent toys, but she should have known better. They bowled along, one behind the other, at the legal speed and in perfect harmony. She smiled at Teddy.

'You're driving very smoothly today. Have you got used to the gears?'

He grinned cheerfully, but she was glad to see that he didn't take his attention away from the road while he answered.

'I'm a quick learner, and this car is fun to drive. I'm thinking about flying lessons next.'

She never forgot that drive. A big golden sun was beginning to sink far out to sea as they drove past the iconic silhouette of Blackpool Tower and then onto the motorway that led north to the Lake District. The countryside was at its early summer best. The grass and the leaves bloomed fresh and green, hawthorn blossom foamed in the hedgerows. The summer air was warm and mild on her face. Thanks to Harold's thoughtfulness, she could enjoy the sensation of the wind flowing past rather than worrying about her hair! He seemed to know a lot about women.

'Does Harold date a lot?' she asked Teddy.

'He takes woman out all the time, but not with much enthusiasm. His parents make him date. They provide an endless stream of girls because they are anxious for him to marry and produce another little duke.'

'Duke!' Cherry squealed. 'You didn't tell me he was a duke! Shouldn't I have curtsied or said 'your grace' or something?'

'He's just a person, Cherry. He's not

the duke at the moment, his father holds the title, but aristocrats like to have a solid line of boys to be sure of the succession.'

'Like farmers,' she agreed. 'My dad wasn't happy until he had a couple of boys in the family.'

'Tough for girls,' Teddy suggested.

'Oh, I don't know. I like horses very much, but I'm not interested in the rest of the farm. It's incredibly hard work and because he had the boys to help him, I was free to do what I wanted. Didn't your father want you to farm?'

'Luckily I've got another brother, and he loves the life.'

'Is your brother older or younger?'

'He's younger than me.'

'So the farm is yours, really?'

'I paid off the mortgage as soon as I started earning, but I've put the property in my brother's name. I'd like to live somewhere warmer, to be honest.'

'Think of relaxing by a swimming pool in the sunshine,' she mused. 'Who wouldn't love that?'

From her seat next to him, she could see the attractive wrinkles that formed at the sides of his eyes every time he gave that cheerful grin.

'You got it! Do you think Spain might be a good place to live? Harold says the the Balearic islands would suit me.'

'I've never been there,' Cherry told him, feeling regretful! 'I've been working too hard to think much about holidaying.'

'We have that in common,' Teddy told her. 'It's good to work hard, but I'm looking forward to having free time.'

The road began to twist and wind its way along the side of a calm and peaceful stretch of water. A glorious red sun glinted on the ripples of the lake. Teddy turned off for the restaurant, which overlooked the lake. The car park was almost full when they got there, and lights blazed from every window of the old stone pub. The bar area was

packed with people, all talking frantically, and every table seemed to be
taken. A huge colour photograph on the
wall of the head chef and owner went
some way to explaining the place's
popularity.

'I've seen the chef's television programmes,' Cherry said to the others as
a waiter seated them at the best table by
a window that overlooked a lake. 'I love
them. Have you seen them?'

'I only watch me soaps,' Angelina
said.

Harold shook his head.

'I don't waste my time with television. Such a depressing quantity of
frightful rubbish is broadcast these
days.'

Cherry winced.

'I'd better tell you now that I work
for a television company. It's called
Prize Television.'

'Surely you could do something
nobler with your life than producing the
kind of twaddle that goes out on
television!' Harold pronounced loftily.

'You snob!' cried an incensed voice. Teddy glared at Harold. 'Don't you hate it when people sneer at your money-making activities without understanding the first thing about business? Go on, if you're so smart, tell us what programmes Cherry makes and exactly what is rubbishy about them?'

Cherry and Angelina exchanged a swift anxious glance as the men argued, wondering if the evening were about to be ruined, but suddenly Harold grinned at his old school friend and said, 'Touché!'

Then Harold turned to Cherry, and she saw true penitence in his grey eyes.

'I'm sorry, Cherry, that was crass of me. What kind of programmes do you make?'

'Trivial ones, but I hope not rubbish,' she told him.

Her companions seemed so interested and asked so many questions about the format for Pony Princesses that she revealed more than usual about

91

her passion for the show. 'The educational side is hidden in the fun,' she finished, 'But it's there all right. In fact, much as people dismiss television,' and she gave Harold a laughing glance, 'it's my sincere belief that even the most popular shows can be life changing.'

'It's true, is that,' Angelina confided. 'It was always a bit mad round at our house, and I used to look at people on the telly and think it doesn't have to be mad. I'm going to better meself and live a nice life.'

Cherry smiled warmly at her.

'And now you're a qualified accountant! That's impressive!'

Angelina's turquoise eyes sparkled with pure pleasure.

'And look at me, sitting in a proper posh restaurant. It's lovely here.'

They stopped talking to read the menus and order. Teddy chose a red wine, which was as smoothly red and powerful as dragon's blood. A single sip warmed you to your toes and made the senses tingle. As soon as the starters came, Harold returned the conversation to the business side of television.

'How is achievement calculated? Is it a matter of ratings?'

'Yes, and awards and media interest as shown by coverage in the papers are important. One key aspect is probably sales to other television stations because that generates income for the company. The most important industry show is being held in Cannes this week, so when I get back to the office I'll know how well my programme has done.'

Harold's eyebrows shot up.

'I think I'd want to be in France this week, supervising my venture'

'I wanted to go,' Cherry sighed.

She capitulated to the urging of her friends and gave them a slightly edited version of the events that had led her to Seaview Spa.

Harold's eyebrows were waggling furiously as he thought. I wonder if he knows how expressive they are, Cherry wondered, smiling to herself. He almost talks with his brows!

Teddy jumped in first.

'This boss of yours is swindling you, Cherry.'

The dark brows lowered now as Harold reached his conclusion.

'Teddy's right.'

Angelina agreed.

'He sounds like a proper rat!'

'There's nothing dishonest about Alan. I've worked for him for three years. He wouldn't be so high up in the company if he was a cheat.'

Teddy touched her hand.

'Are you sure?'

It was hard to crush the optimism in his brown eyes, but Cherry was confident.

'I'm positive.'

Teddy fell silent, but Harold hadn't finished.

'You are definitely being exploited. I know one's not supposed to ask, but think of me as your business manager. What is your salary?'

Cherry felt the friendship and concern flowing from this unlikely son of a duke, and found she didn't mind telling him.

Teddy beamed at her.

'That's not a bad monthly rate, is it, Harold?'

'No, that figure is my yearly salary,' Cherry had to confess. She knew that her pay wasn't impressive; the lower-rung posts in television were so hotly contested that the companies didn't need to offer high wages.

Harold still had questions.

'Will you get a percentage of the profits if your Pony Princesses pro-gramme is successful?'

'No.'

'You are definitely being exploited.'

'The company trained me, and they take the financial risk if a programme fails,' Cherry pointed out, feeling compelled to defend her employers.

'That's true. That's very true. Let me consider your position. You are trained now, but you have produced one money-earning success which will more than pay the business back for their investment in you. The situation is all square. You could leave now with a clear conscience and work independently. I'll represent you, if you like.'

Beside her she could feel Teddy beaming at his business partner.

'That's a very generous offer. Thank you, Harold. You should accept, Cherry. I know he doesn't look like one, but this man is a total genius.'

'I'll think it over,' Cherry promised.

'Are you working on any new ideas?'

'Yes, a programme about knitting.'

'My grannie used to knit,' Angelina said. 'She was rubbish at it, and she used to witter all the time she was knitting. Her pet budgie could say, 'knit one, purl one, oh drat it!''

When the laughter died down, Teddy turned to Cherry.

'What's your new programme going to be like?'

She'd been hogging the limelight for long enough.

'I'll tell you another time! Let's talk about this delicious food instead.'

'Don't tell your employers anything about ideas you've worked on in your own time until we've had a proper consultation,' Harold warned Cherry, his grey eyes serious. 'Promise?'

And she had to promise before he would turn his attention to his plate.

The food was mouth-watering, and Doctor Poppy would have approved every plateful because course after course was high in vegetables and the famous chef appeared to use practically no cream or butter.

'I must learn to cook,' Teddy said, polishing off a delicious towering confection of iced sorbet, raspberries three ways and black chocolate that was billed as a low-fat, no-sugar pudding.

The meal finished with Italian espresso, hot black and wicked. Teddy noticed Cherry pushing hers away half drunk.

'Still missing sugar?' he asked sympathetically.

'Coffee is horrible without sugar,'

Angelina agreed, pushing her barely-tasted cup to one side. 'I like cream in mine as well.'

Harold's eyebrows signalled his disapproval.

'One doesn't put sugar or cream in espresso!' he pronounced.

'Don't be so snobby,' Teddy advised his old friend kindly. 'You drink your coffee any way you like, Angelina.'

But his championship was wasted. She turned adoring turquoise eyes on Harold.

'Harold knows what's right,' she announced. 'I'm never having sugar in my espresso again.'

A pink flush suffused Harold's cheeks and he looked pleased as he smiled down at Angelina. A sudden suspicion gripped Cherry. Could a relationship be blossoming? Well, why not? The ghostlike aristocrat and the bubbly Liverpudlian made an odd couple, but then the four of them made an odd group, yet she'd never had such an enjoyable evening in her life. The well-run restaurant made a delightful setting, and every detail of the food and service had been perfect, but it was more than that. The evening had flashed by in a harmony that was at once both comfortable and vibrant and exciting. The synergy between their little group was perfect. The others seemed to agree with her. They were all reluctant to leave, but the place was closing and the waiter, although he assured them they were welcome to have more drinks in the bar, looked tired.

'We'd better make a move,' Teddy sighed, waving aside offers to pay. 'Waiter, could you bring the bill please?'

'We must have another meal together before your time at the spa finishes,' Harold said, standing up to leave.

Angelina turned beaming turquoise eyes up to his face.

'That'd be lovely!' she breathed.

Teddy looked at Cherry a little anxiously.

'Would you like to come out with us again?'

'I'd love to,' she replied honestly. 'But you must let me pay next time.'

Teddy's smile was enormous. She couldn't help smiling back.

'You can pay the third time we go out,' he told her, a laugh in his brown eyes. 'It's Harold's turn to pickup the bill next time.'

'On the contrary, speaking in my capacity as a business expert, I should call it a very sound strategy to allow Cherry to pay for the second meal.'

'I'll pay for the one after that, so you can pay for meal number four, Harold,' Angelina chipped in.

He greeted the suggestion with enthusiasm.

'First-rate! That suggests that we'll be partaking of four meals together.'

Laughing and teasing, they walked out into a beautiful summer evening. It was still so warm that they put the tops down on the convertible cars again, Angelina clapping her hands at the cleverness of the automatic systems. The two sports cars started off in convoy, but Teddy soon stopped at a viewpoint overlooking the lake and turned off the car lights. At first it seemed dark, but then Cherry's vision adjusted and she could see millions of stars blazing in the black velvet of the sky, and their reflections rippling in the grey water of the lake. The smell of grass floated into the car. A fox barked on the lakeside and an owl hooted.

'It's a beautiful evening,' she said softly.

Teddy turned to look at her.

'It's more than beautiful; it's special, because I'm with you.'

There isn't a subtle bone in his body, Cherry thought, he's bound to try to kiss me now.

But after looking at her for a long, electric moment, he turned on the ignition and reversed the sports car back onto the road. Cherry felt oddly let down. She struggled with her feelings as they drove back to the spa.

She was promised to Alan, of course, and she didn't believe in cheapening kisses by giving them to one man while she was involved with another. But she felt regretful, because she'd had very little experience of kissing, and who knew when she'd be in such a perfect situation again?

5

The next days at the spa flew past. Cherry became unexpectedly fascinated with yoga. At first she thought she was going to hate it. Serena could bend like a rubber band while Cherry couldn't even find the correct muscle to move.

'It's like trying to waggle my ears!' she initially complained. 'It's no good, Serena. My body is too stiff. I can't do it.

But Serena had a million little tricks for coaxing movement out of reluctant bodies, and to her astonishment, Cherry found that she could stretch her muscles after all. And how good it felt!

'I feel as if I'm getting to know my own body,' she said, trying to explain the appeal of the discipline. I'm going to keep on with it. Serena's given me a list of qualified teachers.'

Sukie liked yoga as well because the

pace was gentle and it relieved her stiffness. Angelina and Teddy both adored swimming, especially Teddy. Cherry and Sukie had gotten out of the pool, but he was still ploughing up and down and they stood in a little group, watching his sleek form carving through the brilliant blue water.

'He's like a seal in the water,' Ryan told them, beaming approvingly at his protégée. 'I never knew anyone learn to swim so fast.'

Teddy swam up to the side of the pool and leaned his arms on the edge so that he could talk to them. Crystal drops cascaded down his powerful shoulders.

'Swimming is brilliant!' he announced, his brown eyes sparkling with glee. 'I'm going to have a pool in my house.'

'Where is your house?' Ryan asked.

'I haven't got one yet. I'm going to look around for the perfect place. I was thinking of a ranch somewhere warm with lots of horses. Kentucky maybe, or Australia. Ryan, how many laps a day would keep a man fit?'

'Thirty would do it, in a pool this size.'

'I'll be super-fit then, because I've done sixty laps today!'

Teddy, Sukie and Cherry went in for lunch together. Angelina joined them a few minutes later. The four of them had formed the habit of sitting at a table together for meals. Angelina was uncharacteristically subdued.

'Doctor Poppy says I've got to give up smoking,' she explained. 'I think it's going to be dead hard. I love me fags.'

'I've got complete faith in you,' Teddy announced, smiling as he got up from the table. 'You can do it. I'm going into the bookshop in town. Sukie, you said that you had some shopping to do. Would you like a lift?'

'No, no. Thank you, dear, but I'd slow you down.'

'I'd like the company.'

'Then, yes, please, dear, although, I may not be able to force my old bones into that lovely sports car of yours.'

'And this is the woman who can do the best back bend in the yoga class? You won't have any trouble getting into my car. Don't worry. I'll help you.'

'He's a lovely man,' Angelina said, watching him walk towards the door at the right pace for Sukie. 'He's proper kind, isn't he?'

Cherry had to agree.

'And he's crazy about you,' Angelina continued. 'You are lucky.'

'Oh, I don't think he's serious.'

'Don't be soft, Cherry. He's nuts about you. Surely this other man at your office can't be nicer than Teddy. What's he like?'

'He's very good-looking, and he's the head of the department I work for.'

'Yeah, but what's he like outside of work?'

'I don't know. I guess I'll find out when we start dating.'

Angelina's brow furrowed.

'He never took you out before?'

'He didn't notice me until last week.'

'And then he said he'd fancy you if you lost weight?'

'It wasn't like that. I said that I would diet for the sake of my career.' Cherry remembered the shadowy office, how thrilled she'd been when Alan said that he wanted to see her and actually named the time and place for their first date. She defended him. 'It's more that we were talking about my changing, and he suddenly seemed to see me as a woman for the first time.'

Angelina shook her red head.

'You don't want to go out with a picky man. Picky men always keep picking at you. You'll never be good enough for him. Teddy thinks you're perfect. That's lovely, that is.'

'I'm trying not to encourage him.'

'He's proper chasing you anyway.'

'I'll never see him again after the makeover. He'll forget me quickly enough.'

'I wouldn't be so sure,' Angelina told her. 'He's bonkers about you.'

Cherry wanted to change the subject.

'What about you? Is there anyone special?'

'No, but I want to meet someone. I want to marry a nice man and settle down and have kids. I want to live in a nice house and have lots of kids.'

'Would Harold make good husband material?'

The turquoise eyes filled with sudden pain.

'Not for me! I'm too common. Harold could never marry me.'

'Don't say that! You'd make him a lovely wife!'

Angelina touched Cherry's hand briefly.

'You're a good mate, Cherry, but you're being soft again.'

Angelina ended the conversation by getting quickly to her feet. She glanced at the table as she turned.

'Hey! You've drunk all your coffee! Is it starting to taste better?'

Cherry regarded the empty cup in surprise.

'Just desperate for caffeine, I think,

although you're right, my coffee didn't seem to taste so bitter today. Where are you off to?'

'I'm going to see Moira the makeover lady again. Moira's a proper genius, isn't she? I want a new frock to go dancing in. Are you coming to Blackpool Tower with us on Friday?'

Cherry grinned.

'Yes, and I'm booked in for a makeover session before we go. I can't dance a step, but that's not going to stop me having a new dress.'

* * *

Summer or not, the skies had been grey and a lot of rain had fallen over the last few days, but now Cherry looked through a window and saw that the clouds were lifting. The sun flashed out from behind the creamy piles of cloud. I'll get some fresh air, she decided. She threw on her new pink tracksuit. She would never have chosen pink, but Moira had come up with a set of cards in a rainbow of colours that she said Cherry should wear, and convinced her that a shade of dark pink called Chinese Peony would suit her to perfection. Cherry looked in the mirror and had to admit the woman was right. The dusky pink suited her skin tone and it made her hazel eyes shine and her curls look blonder.

Cherry laced up her trainers, which were also new. She'd bought them because Moira had insisted that she'd be walking much more from now on. She ran down the stairs (Ryan and Doctor Poppy had very strong views on the evils that resulted from using lifts instead of legs!) and crossed the road to the beach.

She turned in the direction of Blackpool's little airport. She'd been told that it was fun to watch the planes soaring over the sand dunes, and it made a good turning point as well, being exactly one mile from the spa.

The hard golden sand stretched for miles and it was completely flat, exactly right for walking. The beach was so broad that there was plenty of space between the people out playing or exercising, so Cherry was able to fall into a vigorous rhythm, striding out without having to watch her step or dodge passersby.

The salt air was still a bit chilly, but it was invigorating, too, and Cherry realised that she felt wonderful. She relished the glow that came from feeling fit. She couldn't help having a job that meant she sat in a chair all day, but she'd promised Doctor Poppy to keep up with her yoga, and to take one brisk walk a week.

'I think you'll find that you feel a great deal better if you stick with the programme,' Poppy had said, looking over her gold spectacles in her characteristic manner. 'Virtue is its own reward.'

She was right, I feel terrific! Cherry thought. At least, her body did. If only she felt as good inside. Inside she felt confused. She had so little experience of relationships with men that it felt overwhelming to be thinking about two men at once!

Alan was the unobtainable ideal she'd secretly pined for all the time she'd worked in television. He was the blond-haired, blue-eyed god who represented everything she wanted: class, sophistication, success. He was a part of the in-crowd in the television world. Now that he'd finally taken notice of her and asked her out, why was she even thinking about a man who was Alan's exact opposite in every possible way?

Yet for all Teddy's gaucheness, his enthusiasm and enjoyment of life were infectious. She liked him. She liked his cheerful bluntness and the way it was tempered by sensitivity and a natural consideration for other people. She knew that he liked her, and she couldn't help enjoying the feeling. He was good to be around

A helicopter buzzed low overhead and vanished over the sand dunes.

She'd walked a whole mile and reached the airport without even noticing. The high ridges of the dunes hid the runways. The gulls, the wind and the waves were so loud that she couldn't hear any engines, only the roar of the ocean. She looked around the long flat beach and wondered if there would be any more aircraft. As she was peering around, a young golden Labrador dog scampered over to her, its tail wagging. Cherry put out a hand.

'Hello. You're gorgeous, aren't you?'

'If only women greeted me like that,' said a panting male voice as the dog's owner rushed up. 'I'm sorry. She's only a pup and not trained yet. Did Goldie jump up at you?'

He clipped the lead on to his puppy's collar as he was speaking.

'She didn't jump up,' Cherry assured him.

He straightened and grinned. He was a nice, friendly-looking man of about her own age, comfortably casual in jeans and a corduroy jacket.

'Are you plane spotting? The three-fifteen for Majorca leaves in a couple of minutes. It's a Boeing 727, one of the big new ones, so it's fun to watch. If you wait here, you'll see it.'

'Would your puppy let me pick her up?'

'There's nothing she'd like better. Goldie loves being made a fuss of.'

Cherry scooped up the warm bundle of golden fur. The puppy seemed to like being cuddled. It wagged its tail and licked her nose. The next few minutes flew past what with patting the puppy and chatting easily. Cherry forgot that she was waiting to see a plane, so she let out a shriek when the great silver machine appeared from behind the sand dunes and flew low over her head, sending waves of hot wind to tumble her blonde curls. The plane flew high, and as it vanished, even over the thunderous engine noise, she heard a distinct clunk as the wheels and landing carriage folded themselves away.

She got her breath back and turned,

laughing, to the puppy owner.

'That was fun! I've never seen a plane from that angle before. I'm glad I didn't miss it, so thanks!'

His gaze was openly admiring.

'You're welcome. I say, you wouldn't like to come and have a cup of coffee with me and Goldie sometime, would you?'

'That's nice of you, but I can't. I'm only here for a few more days and my schedule is packed.'

Cherry gave the adorable puppy a final pat, returned it to its owner and turned to walk back to the hotel. Another man asking her out! What was going on?

Halfway back to Seaview Spa, she admitted that the world wasn't turning on its head, she was. She was more open, more relaxed and friendly, and so people were responding to her differently. She was almost prepared to agree with Poppy. The doctor maintained that Cherry had paid too much attention to the teasing at school. 'The children at school used to call me a skinny bookworm,' she had said crisply, 'and they used to make fun of my flowery name besides, but I didn't take any notice of them. You, I think, were more sensitive. It's a shame, Cherry, that your image of yourself has been formed by a pack of thirteen-year-olds.'

'But your ideas don't hold true in the world of television. I can't be good enough if people are having meetings about me and deciding that I'm too fat to represent the company!'

Poppy's pale blue eyes looked over the brim of her gold spectacles.

'It seems to me that you'll have to decide whether you're going to continue to let yourself be bullied,' was her crisp reply.

Cherry still hadn't decided what she thought by the time she got back to the hotel. While she'd been out, workmen had begun erecting a scaffold over the front of the hotel, and inside, in the lobby, a group of residents was looking at paint charts.

'We're agreed on cream for the stone-work,' Poppy said to her husband. He provided the delicious food at the spa and had come out of his kitchen in his chef's whites. 'Why can't I have burnt orange for the paintwork?'

'Because my favourite, blue, is the classic seaside colour,' he replied. 'Let's take a vote.' He displayed the paint charts. 'What do you think, people? Let's have a show of hands for orange! And now who's going to vote for blue?'

Blue won by a majority of three. Poppy's husband gave her a hug.

'Blue it is. With all the salt in the air, we'll have to repaint every year. If you don't like the colour, next year we'll go orange, I promise.'

Dinner was even more delicious than usual, and Cherry surprised herself by drinking every drop of her coffee and enjoying it. Her taste buds seemed to have become more efficient. Her salad zinged with flavour, and she could taste every nuance of her iced peach parfait.

'Have you noticed anything about

your sense of taste?' she asked the others. She was sitting with Sukie, Teddy and Angelina as usual.

They all had, especially Angelina, who had nicotine patches all up her arms, but hadn't had a cigarette since her interview with Doctor Poppy.

'I can smell flowers now,' she told them. 'I never knew freesias had a smell!'

Sukie and Angelina left, but Teddy delayed.

'How is your idea of a knitting programme progressing?'

'Not very fast,' Cherry confessed. 'I am struggling to make an exciting format. There's not much drama in saying, 'You have three months to knit a sweater and your time starts NOW'!'

Knitting is one of those hobbies that people either love or hate with equal ferocity! A surprising number of people were passionate about the pastime, but an almost equivalent number thought it was old-fashioned and dull. Cherry, who was in the passionate camp, wanted to change the image of knitting, but how? As she talked, Cherry expected Teddy's eyes to glaze over with boredom, but he continued to chat with her, an hour sped by, and she became aware of the quality of his mind. He asked questions that weren't obvious. He made her think. He gave her ideas.

'Shall we continue this conversation while we walk on the beach?' he asked her.

The expression in his eyes scared her. She could see so much liking and enthusiasm in his face. It wasn't fair to lead him on, and besides, she could feel that golden lifting sensation at the base of her skull that told her a brainwave was on its way.

'No, thank you.' She could see he was about to argue, so she added, 'You've motivated me! I want to go to my room and make notes while the muse is with me.'

This he seemed to respect, leaving her at once with a smile.

And it was true. She was inspired.

That evening and all the next morning ideas poured out of her brain and into her laptop, and by lunchtime she was able to tell her companions that she had a perfectly-worked out formula for her new show.

'I'm sure it will be a huge success, dear,' Sukie told her. 'I never miss the baking programme, or the sewing contest. It's good to see the old skills being revived. When I was a girl we made all our own clothes and I used to enjoy it.'

The next item on their programme was a trip to Blackpool Tower for an afternoon tea dance. Only one couple at the spa could already dance, but Poppy had assured the rest of them that many people went to watch and to enjoy the ambience at the famous venue.

'I hope some of you will be encouraged to explore dancing as a form of exercise, but please don't get too carried away by the afternoon tea,' she warned.

When they got to the Tower Ball-room, tiered cake plates adorned many of the tables around the dance floor.

'I see what Poppy means about the wicked cakes,' Sukie said.

'We could get a drink each and share the scones,' Angelina suggested.

And that's what they did. Although everyone from the spa was at the ballroom, as usual, the four of them were sitting together. A waitress in traditional black and white costume fetched them tea in a rose-printed china teapot. Then she brought a triple-tiered cake stand that displayed miniature cucumber sandwiches, prawn vol-au-vents and a selection of cakes. Even a generous portion of scones with straw-berry jam and cream was not too wicked when shared between four.

'I love this place,' Angelina said, with her usual enthusiasm, looking around at the grand old ballroom. It had lavish plasterwork, a painted ceiling, brilliant chandeliers and of course that famous sprung dance floor, but there was no denying that the venue was showing its age. It was faded and dusty. The magnificent ballroom looked very much more attractive when the lights were lowered to a golden glow and the music started. A man began playing a tune on a brown organ. Secretly Cherry thought it looked rather dull and wondered why the Blackpool Tower Organ was so famous.

Teddy's eyes were thoughtful.

'I love the plaster cherubs, but they could do with refurbishing.'

'Everything in this room would be all the better for a good clean,' Sukie agreed.

Teddy nodded.

'But it would be a thorny exercise. How would you get up to the ceiling? And look at the size of the chandeliers! I wonder how difficult it would be to wash each of those glass tear drops?'

'Think of the hours of labour it would take, dear! It would cost a fortune in wages.'

Teddy nodded thoughtfully at Sukie.

'You know, there should be a way to automate housework.'

He and Sukie got into a complicated discussion that mixed mathematics and the price of cleaning materials which only broke off when a fanfare sounded and the organ that had been playing background music began to descend into the floor of one side of the stage and a stunning white organ rose from the other side and whirled around to face the room.

'This is more exciting!' Cherry cried, joining in the clapping that met its appearance.

The dance began. The organist played a lilting Viennese Waltz and a swarm of dancers took to the floor. Some people were expert dancers, even professional. Sukie recognised a couple she'd seen dancing on television. Most people were at a medium standard, they whirled around the floor neither showing off nor disgracing themselves, and a few beginners bumbled around causing the occasional traffic jam, but nobody seemed to mind, and all of the dancers seemed to be enjoying themselves hugely.

'Oh, I wish I could dance!' Angelina cried in rapture. 'I am so going to learn.'

Teddy turned to Cherry. He was wearing his new clothes with assurance, and she suddenly realised what a fine figure of a man he was.

'Can you dance?' he asked her.

'No.'

'Neither can I. I wish I could. I'd like to sweep you up in my arms and dance you into paradise.'

The intensity in his brown eyes made her breathless.

'I thought you didn't know how to talk to women.'

'It's you,' he said softly. 'It's easy to talk to you. I look at you and simply tell you what I feel.'

She met his eyes for a long, long, second, and then she turned away, feeling breathless.

'Oh! Here's Harold,' Cherry cried in

surprise, spotting a grey, stork-like figure drifting slowly towards their table. She had begun to suspect that he came to the spa to see Angelina rather than check up on Teddy, and now she was sure of it. Why, he'd been with them only yesterday and they weren't expecting to see him again until the day after tomorrow.

'He always makes me think of a heron,' she said to Teddy.

'It's odd you should say that! There's a heron on the family shield.'

'Hi everyone,' Harold said as he reached the table. He may have addressed everyone, but his eyes were on one person only.

Caught unawares, Angelina looked up with naked joy in her turquoise eyes. Harold looked at her loving expression for a long moment, and then, like a piece of paper when a match is put to it, he seemed to burn and take light. He was radiant with pleasure.

Sukie looked at the couple, who seemed to be locked in an enchanted bubble, then she looked at Teddy and Cherry.

'I don't want to be a gooseberry,' she said, starting to struggle to her feet.

But Teddy jumped up and found an empty table which he placed between them and the rest of the spa guests. He then arranged the chairs so that they all sat in one large group, and then he bought absolutely everyone a drink or more cakes, whatever they wanted, so that Sukie was effortlessly absorbed into the general jollities.

You can't join in with ballroom dances like the quickstep or the foxtrot without knowing the steps, and the fast Latin dances looked even more complicated, but every so often the music changed to the languorous rhythm of a rumba, and Teddy wasn't slow to notice that a few couples swayed happily on the outside edges of the wooden dance floor, oblivious to the more accomplished displays in the centre of the room.

The next time a slow number played,

he stood up and held out a hand to Cherry.

'Dance with me?' he asked.

It was as if her feet decided for her. She was standing up and walking towards him before she could open her mouth to say no. His strong arms held her tight. She lifted her arms and put her hands on his forearms. He had nice arms, they were firm and she could feel the muscles that his swimming was developing under the crisp cotton of his shirt. He moved well. Her own understanding of musical rhythms wasn't developed, but she knew enough to sense that his was spot on.

His shoulder was exactly the right height to rest her head on, and she had to fight the urge to let her head drop and relax. She was afraid, she realised. She was afraid to let go and melt into his arms. When had she ever allowed herself the luxury of leaning on a man? Be honest! When had the support ever been offered? The sensation was completely new.

Teddy put one hand under her chin and tilted it so that his brown eyes looked directly at her.

'Unwind,' he said gently, his expression soft and happy. 'I can't dance, but I promise I won't drop you.'

And once more her body took over, relaxing into his arms like a flower twining around a tree. He felt warm, strong, utterly comforting. The gentle music lulled her and she felt as blissful as a baby dreaming in its cot. It was intoxicating to be a part of the dance, rather than watching from the sidelines. She felt alive, whole and happy. Lights whirled around her and then slowed as the tune came to an end.

Teddy looked at her and smiled.

'You feel so good in my arms.'

The white organ gave the fanfare that announced another song, and Cherry was glad they played two of each kind of dance. Locked in one another's arms, she and Teddy twirled and rocked at the edge of the dance floor, moving to a rhythm as gentle and natural as waves on a beach. Cherry was sad when the second dance ended and the music changed to a dramatic tango.

Teddy looked at her with a smile in his eyes.

'Will you come for a walk on the beach with me?'

Cherry looked over towards where their group had been sitting. There was no sign of Angelina and Harold, and Sukie was chatting to a pleasant couple from the Midlands.

'Why not?' she breathed.

The bright space outside was a shock after the dimness of the ballroom. Gulls screamed in the blue sky, they could hear the thump of fairground music, and the afternoon sun was a warm kiss on their faces. She felt better than she had for years.

'Mm, that candyfloss smells good!' Teddy said.

She laughed.

'I'd rather have a hotdog.'

'Really?'

'No, not really. I'd rather feel good.'

'Me too,' he said in surprise as they crossed the road and headed for the beach. 'I don't think my local takeaway do vegetables. I will have to learn to cook!'

It seemed natural for him to take her hand as they turned in the direction of the spa.

'Is it too far for you to walk back?' Teddy asked her. 'We can get the tram if you feel tired.'

'It's only a mile,' Cherry said, then laughed. 'I have changed. I wouldn't have dreamed of attempting a mile this time last month.'

'I've changed, too,' Teddy told her.

His pace slowed, and he drew her towards a wooden breakwater. He sat first, and somehow Cherry found herself on his knee. He felt so good. His body was strong and warm and supportive. They looked at one another with uncertainly.

'I promised Alan,' she said, looking at the sand below her feet. She picked up a shell and turned it over. It was slightly worn by the sea, but pretty pearl colours still gleamed in its depths.

The silence became uneasy. She was finding it hard to breathe. She looked up and met Teddy's brown eyes. He was watching her with infinite patience and understanding.

'I'm glad that I met you,' he said. 'I feel that I've made trouble for you, and I want you to be happy, but I can't regret having met you.'

He's sweeter than a cup of coffee with sugar, she thought, looking at his face. He wasn't afraid to be open. He was letting her see how much he wanted her, and to be wanted so much is powerfully seductive.

'I want you the way you are, Cherry. I don't want you to be thinner, or more successful. Can you say that about this other man?'

Then he put up a hand and touched her parted lips with one finger. 'Sorry! That was the wrong question to ask you. I've thought of a better one. How would you like an old flame to make him jealous?'

He stroked the blonde curls that tumbled in the sea breeze.

'That doesn't work, either,' he said sadly, before Cherry could answer. 'I don't want to play tricks and be clever, Cherry. If you don't want to kiss me freely then we had better keep walking.'

He opened his arms, as if expecting her to get off his knee and walk on. Cherry was surprised by her own reluctance to move.

She felt him catch his breath. His brown eyes held a world of warmth.

'Cherry?' he questioned softly.

She angled her head so she was facing him, moved closer so that their lips were near enough to touch. He pulled her closer and she felt the warmth and strength of his chest. She could feel his heartbeat. The intimacy alarmed her. She pulled back and quickly checked his expression. There was nothing but love and goodwill in his eyes. With a sigh, she relaxed into his arms once more. He made no move, and she understood that he was waiting for her. She leaned into his warmth so that her lips made teasing contact with his. She moved back slightly, but this time he lunged for her and his mouth took hers firmly. The touch of his lips on hers felt like destiny. She'd wished for this kiss, yet the reality surprised her. Their kiss felt like a dreamy moonlight fantasy, but the warmth of the daylight sun on their bodies was real. The gulls screaming in the air above them were real, as was the sound of the flow of the sea water that roared in the distance and the touch of the breeze as it patted her cheeks.

A kiss is so simple, yet Cherry's reactions were so complex. She felt her arms tighten around Teddy's neck, locking her to him in a velvet embrace, and yet the realisation that her body was reacting without her mind's per-mission was terrifying. The quick tug of desire that zinged around her body was deeply unwelcome. Her reaction to him was past her reckoning. She didn't like being so out of control. Unease overtook pleasure and she rolled out of his arms and stood panting on the sand, looking out to sea.

The distant line of blue where the air met the water blurred as she remembered her promise to Alan. Tears stung her eyes. She would have to let someone down now, whatever she decided, and she knew that she couldn't give up the idea of Alan. He'd been her idol for too long. She'd never had any intention of breaking their proposed date, so why in the world was she dallying with Teddy? How could she have let things go so far? Leading a man on, it was called, and only selfish women did it. They were ugly words for an ugly action.

'I'm sorry. That was selfish of me.'

'Don't be sorry. I enjoyed kissing you!'

'I'm ashamed of myself.'

He walked around so that he stood between her and the sea.

'Hey, don't cry.'

'I promised Alan.'

'Blame it on me,' Teddy advised her cheerfully, his brown eyes serene. 'Don't be so serious, darling. It was only a kiss, and you've never even dated this man yet. It can't matter so much.'

'I've loved Alan for three years! How could I risk throwing away my big chance for . . . '

'For a mere kiss with me?' Teddy said, a tinge of anger in his voice.

'I shouldn't have kissed anyone, let alone . . . '

'Let alone boring old Teddy!'

Now he sounded sad as well as angry, but it wouldn't help matters if she'd told him that she was feeling guilty about kissing a man that she liked. It was easier to let him assume the worst.

'I didn't mean it that way.'

'Why not? You are right! It's a big mistake to kiss a stupid man who has no clue about women.'

'You're not stupid!'

'I'm stupid enough to fall for the first woman I meet.'

What a mess — she so didn't want to hurt him. At least she'd been honest, she'd warned him.

'I told you about Alan. I told you that I didn't come here to meet a man.'

His brown eyes met her hazel gaze. There was no admiration now, only pain and anger.

'Did you enjoy kissing me? Tell me that. Did you enjoy our kiss?'

The word 'yes' floated into her mind, but the truth would only make things worse.

'No.'

'I don't believe you,' he cried furiously.

'Teddy, please. Please let's not argue.'

She watched as he controlled himself. It seemed to take a titanic effort, but he managed it. The face he turned towards her was calm, but tight and his eyes were cold.

'I'm sorry that I upset you, Cherry. It was not my intention and I shan't bother you again.'

He turned to leave her, and, perversely, she felt as if she were losing her one true friend in the world. Then he turned back and spoke with more of his accustomed energy.

'I've got something badly wrong here. You know I don't have a lot of experience with women, but I'm a quick learner, Cherry, and I'm good at problem solving. Our relationship is not going to end here.'

'It must!'

'Oh, no. I'll work it out.'

'Human hearts are more complicated than mathematical numbers.'

'I'm beginning to realise that,' he replied grimly.

And this time he did turn and leave her.

6

The long hot shower she took before bed didn't wash away the memory of the heartbreak in his eyes, and Cherry spent an uncomfortable night. As well you deserve to, she told herself. It was probably her own lack of experience that had led her into this tangle. Teddy had made it clear enough that he liked her, but she'd never followed that thought through and realised that she could hurt him.

The next morning she didn't want to face him. She dallied in her room until she was in danger of being late for yoga. She thought that she would avoid Teddy by scampering in at the last moment, but he'd had the same idea and they collided in the doorway.

'Sorry!'

'Sorry!'

They spread their mats on opposite

sides of the room, but she was achingly aware of him all though the class.

At breakfast he sat at another table. Sukie looked at his distant figure, and then she looked at Cherry with grandmotherly green eyes.

'Oh, dear. The course of true love never runs smooth. I thought you two were getting on so well.'

Cherry remembered their kiss.

'Too well.'

The grandmotherly look sharpened.

'How much too well?'

'Just a kiss,' Cherry assured her, 'but I promised Alan not to get mixed up with anyone else while I was away. It's funny, Sukie. I've never really had a boyfriend. I never expected to meet someone at the spa. I thought Alan was crazy, making me promise to stay free for him. I never dreamed I'd get entangled with another man.'

'Are you engaged to this Alan?'

She had to laugh at the question.

'No, we haven't even had a date yet.'

'Well then, that means you are single,

I wouldn't worry about a little kiss. A holiday romance isn't the end of the world. Between you, me and the gatepost, dear, I wouldn't throw Teddy's shoes out of the bedroom.'

'Sukie!'

'Why the shocked face? You'll go a long way to find a better man.'

'You can't be serious. You'd never talk to your own daughters like this!'

'Oh wouldn't I, dear? I'd tell them soon enough if I saw them letting a good man slip through their fingers. No, it's worse than that! You are pushing him away. You're crazy! And I'll tell you something else. I didn't raise any fools. My daughters listened to me, and they are all happily married!'

Cherry was still mulling over Sukie's surprising advice when Teddy walked over to her, very much with the air of a man approaching the hangman.

'May I talk to you for a moment?'

'Of course we can talk.'

The difficulty was to find a private spot. Cherry had no intention of ending up in a bedroom with him, and she was glad that he didn't suggest it. In the end, Teddy led her up to the very top of the stairs and out through the fire escape onto the windy roof of the hotel.

'Wow!' Cherry cried, pushing back her tumbling blonde curls.

The view was so stunning that it demanded attention. They spent a few minutes picking out landmarks. There was the promenade with a tram running past the iconic tower, looking just like a postcard. You could see the whole sweep of the Blackpool beach, including the breakwater where they had kissed. Cherry looked beyond it to the sand dunes that ran towards the pretty town of Formby. Beyond that, you could see the distant hills of the Lake District.

Huge cumulus clouds raced over the sky, sometimes cutting off the sun, sometimes zipping along freely. The clouds cast moving shadows on the sand.

But you couldn't spend the whole

morning saying how gorgeous the weather was and how incredible the view was. Teddy made the first move. He turned towards her.

'I'm sorry about yesterday.'

His brown eyes were steady and mature.

'Me too,' she confessed.

'I'm not sorry I kissed you.'

Cherry shrank away and held up a pleading hand to stop him.

'Don't worry. I'm not going to revisit our previous conversation. But I do want to say that I am sorry it's made things awkward. We promised to go out with Harold and Angelina tonight. Do you think we could pretend to be friends for their sake?'

Cherry had to admire his frankness, his skilful handling of an awkward situation.

'We could make an effort, I suppose.'

'I'd like it if we could really be friends.'

'It's not fair on you.'

She saw a flash of his old smile.

'You let me worry about what's best for me.'

Cherry had a feeling that spending an evening with him wouldn't be that simple. And talking of Angelina and Harold . . . she dug in the pocket of her sweat suit for her phone. There were no messages.

'I haven't seen Angelina since yesterday, and she hasn't texted me. Have you seen Harold?'

'No, now you mention it. He's vanished.'

'I don't think they need our company tonight. I would go if I was needed, but, as it is, I'd rather not go out with you, Teddy.'

'If that's what you would prefer, I'll cancel our reservation.'

He spoke calmly, but the pain in his eyes was telling a different story. It would only make the situation worse if she tried to explain that it wasn't his company she dreaded, but her own tangle of feelings.

'I'm sorry,' Cherry said again.

'And I keep telling you not to be sorry. I want to tell you something else, Cherry. I'll never mention this again because I know you feel differently, but I treasure the moments we had together. If they have to end, well, that's too bad. I know you keep your promises. I want you to promise that if you ever change your mind, you'll let me know.'

'I'll do that.'

'Thank you.'

A silence fell between them. Sunshine streamed down, then vanished as a cold puffy cloud flew over the tops of their heads, casting a shadow. Cherry became aware of the screaming of the gulls. There was no more to say, so why was it so hard to part? They were silent for a long, long minute, and then Teddy moved slightly, and turned to her with a polite expression.

'It's time for swimming. It's not your favourite activity, is it? Are you going to cut class?'

She didn't like the way he was looking at her, as if she was a mere acquaintance, someone he knew slightly and didn't care about. She liked the way he had been. She wanted him to look at her with a world of happiness in his eyes, as if she were the one woman who could make him happy.

What was she thinking? It wasn't Teddy she wanted to look at her that way, it was Alan! She looked away from Teddy's soft brown eyes before answering.

'I'll never learn to swim if I don't keep trying, and I do like being in the water.'

But as she splashed around in the warm water at the shallow end of the pool, watching Teddy complete his self-imposed sixty laps in elegant style, she came to a sudden conclusion. She was going to cut the rest of the classes. She'd had it with the spa. She'd achieved all that she'd come to do: she'd made diet and lifestyle changes she knew that she'd stick to, and she knew that her self-image was changing, although she wasn't sure whether to credit those changes to Moira the makeover lady and Doctor Poppy or to Teddy, but she was finished here.

If she left now she could have a night at home before returning to work. She wanted to go home more than anything in the world. She didn't want to be at the spa anymore, trying to deal with the situation with Teddy. The easiest way to save his feelings was to leave at once.

★ ★ ★

The Hawthorn family had been farming at Hilltop House for over three hundred years. The stone farm house was tucked under the brow of the hill. The house was surrounded by farm buildings, sheep pens and great piles of haylige wrapped in black plastic. The winter feed was important. The moorland grass was sparse and thin in winter. The only trees that grew this high up on the moors were the mountain ash, and the sturdy hawthorn, and those trees that did survive were bent because of the prevailing wind. It could be bleak on a cold day, but Cherry loved her childhood home. There was nowhere more beautiful than the moors in summer with the birds calling overhead.

Cherry's mother threw open the door.

'I heard the car!' Joyce cried, giving her daughter a hug. Her hazel eyes shone with happiness. 'Come on in. I made a Sussex Pond pudding the moment you phoned. I don't know why you always phone and ask if I'm free for your visit. Where else would I be but home?'

'I call so you'll make my favourite pudding,' Cherry answered, giggling.

It was lovely to be in the familiar kitchen. From the delicious smells floating in the air, she deduced that they were having roast lamb for dinner, followed by her favourite suet crust pudding with a whole lemon in the centre of it. Shep the sheepdog was curled up in his basket by the Aga stove. She rushed over to greet him, and her old friend wagged his tail and licked her hand.

'It's wonderful the way he keeps going,' her mother said. 'Cherry, it's lovely to see you. Take off your coat and I'll make us a cup of tea.'

But the moment Cherry took off her coat, her mother's face changed completely. Her hazel eyes widened in shock.

'Good heavens, child! What have you been doing? You're as thin as a skeleton! Are you well?'

'I'm fine, mum,' Cherry told her, taking a cup of tea.

Her mother pushed over the milk jug and the sugar bowl. Cherry ignored them and took a sip of tea.

'You're drinking black tea! Since when have you drunk black tea? Why don't you want milk and sugar? There's no goodness in black tea. Cherry, have you been dieting? Answer me now.'

Cherry was surprised by the sharp, worried tone of her mother's voice.

'I'm not dieting, mum, but I am making a few changes.'

148

Her mother pushed the sugar bowl towards Cherry, and her hands were shaking.

'Take it!'

Cherry pushed the bowl away and her mother looked furious and pushed the sugar back.

'You've got to keep your strength up.'

'She looks strong enough to me,' said a hearty voice behind them.

'Dad!' Cherry cried, turning to meet his hug.

'Now then, our Cherry. You look well. Holidays must suit you. Where was it you went again?'

'Blackpool. I went to a new health spa that's opened there.'

'Health spa?' her mother snapped. 'Fine sort of a health spa that sends you back in this state. You're nothing but a shadow.'

'I haven't been dieting, mum. I haven't tried to lose any weight. If I look a bit trimmer, it's because I'm getting more exercise.'

'I've never seen you look so well for

years, Cherry,' her father said.

And his sentiments were echoed by Cherry's brothers, Alan and Peter, who piled into the kitchen at that moment. Unusually for them, they kissed their sister and told her she looked wonderful.

But Joyce wouldn't be soothed. Her fussy, worried state seemed to increase all the time she was cooking and dishing up, and it boiled over while they were sitting at the dinner table. Cherry's father sat at the head of the table as usual, carving up the roast lamb into generous slices and piling the men's plates high.

'Only one slice of lamb, please, Dad,' Cherry said.

Her father passed her a blue plate with one slice of meat on it without comment, but her mother sprang to her feet.

'One slice isn't enough, Cherry!'

Cherry's mother snatched the carving knife out of her husband's hand, carved a large and jagged slice of meat, and then slung it onto her daughter's plate.

Her husband looked at her with his mouth open.

'Joyce?' he questioned.

'She's too thin! Look at the child! She's skin and bone! You must eat, Cherry.'

Cherry met her mother's eyes feeling uncomfortable. Where had this tense stranger come from? She knew that her mother liked the family to eat well. Joyce was was never happier than when she was filling her family's plates with delicious calorie-laden food. As a child, Cherry had sometimes wished that her mother was the kind of person who understood how important it was for teenagers to be thin, but she'd had a healthy appetite and she liked to please her mother, so she'd never tried to turn down the platefuls that were set in front of her. But now she was grown up, and she'd agreed a plan with Doctor Poppy.

'One slice is plenty, Mum.'

'You must eat every scrap on that

plate!' her mother insisted.

'I can't!' Cherry protested. 'That's far too much meat.'

'Don't you dare leave any of that lamb!' Joyce fairly shrieked.

Cherry's brothers shuffled their feet and looked uncomfortable at this sudden scene. Their mother was usually so tranquil and happy! Their father put a reassuring arm around his wife's shaking shoulders.

'What's upset you, Joyce? This is our little girl, not a hulking farm hand. It stands to reason her appetite won't match ours.'

'She must eat!'

'What's going to happen that's so bad if she doesn't?'

'It's like Phyllis all over again! This is just how it started.'

Joyce burst into tears. The whole family watched her, feeling appalled. She never cried! Cherry's father kept his arms around his wife, giving her soothing little pats as if she were an injured farm animal he were dealing

152

with, and gradually she grew calm.

'No wonder you're upset, love,' he said, understanding.

But their children looked on, confused.

Joyce went over to the pine Welsh dresser that stood against one wall. Dotted among the willow-patterned china were family photographs in frames. She selected a black and white photograph and brought it to the table.

'My little sister, Phyllis,' she said, her voice choked with emotion, pushing the photo over to Cherry. 'She was such an angel, always smiling and happy, but then she got ill.' Tears flowed again, but they were of a different kind. Her unhappy hysteria had melted into a cleansing, healing release of emotion.

Cherry looked at the wistful face of the little blonde girl in the photograph. The portrait had been on the dresser all her life, and she had known vaguely that she'd had another auntie who'd died young, but now she was hearing the true story of the tragedy. Her mother took the photograph back and regarded it sadly.

'She got thinner and thinner. There was nothing we could do. There was nothing anyone could do. If she'd just eat she might stand a chance, the doctor said. But she couldn't.'

'I'm sorry, Mum,' Cherry said.

'I'm sorry, too, love,' her mother said. Her voice was sounding more like her usual self every minute and her eyes were calm again. 'That was then and this is now. You eat what you want to Cherry, love. I'm such a fool.'

'No you're not!' Cherry cried, and she jumped to her feet and gave her mother a hug. Her mother hugged her back hard before insisting on sweeping the plates off the table and reheating dinner.

Happy that the emotional storm was over, the men were quick to change the conversation to farming matters, and soon they were sitting around the kitchen table chatting as if it were a normal meal on a normal day, but

154

Cherry felt as if she been shown a glimpse into a new world. Her mother's story about the past explained a lot about the present, Cherry thought. Now she understood why Joyce had been so happy to see her plump little baby growing into a chubby little girl and then a curvy teenager. Cherry felt very close to her mother as she thanked her for a delicious meal, and she noticed that her normally undemonstrative brothers were being especially loving towards their mother as well.

'What next, Cherry, love?' asked her dad. 'Are you staying for a few days?'

'I've got all day tomorrow,' she answered. 'But it's back to work on Monday.'

She felt a thrill of anticipation. There was a lot to look forward to! She'd find out how Pony Princesses had fared, and there were only three days to go before her date with Alan.

7

'You look well, Cherry!'

'Is that a new dress?'

'Have you lost weight?'

'Did you say you went to a health spa? Give me the address! I want to go there!'

'Thank you,' Cherry said, laughing at the people she shared an office with. 'I would recommend Sea View Spa to anyone.'

Gemma came in with a tray full of tea and coffee cups.

'Cherry!' she squealed. 'You look amazing!'

She distributed the drinks around the various desks.

'I'll have to change the brew list in the kitchen,' Cherry said, looking at the white coffee she'd ended up with. 'I'm not taking milk and sugar in my drinks from now on.'

Gemma smiled in her friendly fashion.

'Do you want a fresh cup?'

'Don't bother. One in the old style won't hurt me,' Cherry said, turning on her computer.

She reached for her drink while she waited for the machine to boot up. She was secretly looking forward to a proper cup of coffee, her first for over two weeks, but no sooner than she taken a big mouthful than her face screwed up in disgust. All she could taste was sugar. It was like drinking milk-flavoured syrup. Shuddering she pushed her mug aside. Goodbye to her old ways! She leapt to her feet, rushed to the kitchen, made a fresh drink and changed the details against her name on the list on the wall.

Back at her desk she took a sip of delicious black coffee and rolled up her sleeves. The in-tray was overflowing with minutes and memos, her email system was warning her that it had no more memory and it was going to stop working if she didn't clear out some of the 495 emails that were clogging it up, and her desk was covered in sticky yellow notes. It was good to be back!

She hadn't been working long when a stir ran around the office. The internal walls were made of glass, which was good because you could see people coming.

'It's Alan Jenkins!' hissed Gemma, reaching into her bag for her favourite perfume spray. A powerful scent of jasmine and musk filled the office.

Cherry felt her heart thumping in anticipation, but she kept her eyes fixed on her screen, pretending not to be excited as the door opened and Alan walked in.

'Alan, I've finished typing this outline for you,' simpered Emma.

'Alan, I've designed the slides for your presentation,' Gemma said, smiling.

'Alan, I've got your research for you,' cooed Sally.

He brushed them all aside and

headed straight for Cherry, perching himself elegantly on the corner of her desk. His slim legs were crossed at exactly the right angle, displaying polished leather loafers. It might be first thing on a Monday morning, but he was dressed to impress. His jeans were neatly pressed. His cotton shirt was crisp and natty cuff links peeped out from below the sleeves of his blazer.

Cherry looked up and wondered if she could be fantasising. Surely the most desirable man in the world couldn't be sitting on the edge of her desk, smiling at her?

'Did you have a nice holiday?' he asked, showing his white teeth as his smile grew even wider.

She felt herself melting. Why, he was even better looking than she remembered. Once or twice during her time at the spa, she'd wondered if he could possibly be as gorgeous as the image she carried around with her, but here was the reality, and he was wonderful!

Alan flicked his perfectly streaked fringe out of his eyes. His grin was utterly boyish and charming.

'Hello? Earth to Cherry?'

Oh! She was daydreaming. She felt her cheeks growing hot as she mumbled a reply.

'I had a lovely time, thanks.'

It is hard to think straight with such gorgeous blue eyes boring into you! Cherry knew that her thought processes were growing fuzzy but her work was important to her. She was desperate to know if her programme was popular.

'How did Pony Princesses do?' she said, and the exact same time that Alan opened his mouth and said:

'I hope you accomplished a final format on your new programme.'

They both laughed, but Alan recovered first.

'You brief me about your new programme and then I'll give you the data.'

She wished she could be more cool and sophisticated, but she was avid to know how her format had fared at the trade show.

'Please tell me about Pony Princesses. I can't bear to wait.'

Cherry felt her hopes rising as she met his blue eyes and registered his jubilant expression, but he still said nothing. He was teasing her, making her wait.

'Please!' she begged.

A smug smile split his face.

'It couldn't have been a more profitable trip. Our show was the hit of the Festival. The format sold to every country.'

A warming, golden glow spread around Cherry's heart. Her ability was vindicated! Now she had a track record, people would forget she was a secretary who hadn't been to university. With a success under her belt, she'd be able to put forward her ideas without needing a sponsor.

She smiled up at the man who'd made it all possible with her heart in her eyes.

'Thanks, Alan. Thanks for promoting my programme.'

'I'd be happy to take your ideas forward at any time, Cherry.' His blue eyes twinkled as he continued, 'But you can't rest on your laurels, Cherry. You know that television is all about your next success. I hope you've been progressing your new format. What do you have to report?'

Cherry opened her mouth, and then paused as a picture of Harold popped into her mind. She closed her mouth while she considered her promise. The business-minded duke had advised her to say nothing about her new format, but surely he was being too cautious? Alan had always been her biggest supporter and, to be honest, she was looking forward to impressing him! She knew he'd be delighted to hear that the format was fully developed. She smiled and opened her mouth again.

'Well, as it happens . . . '

She broke off. Over Alan's shoulder she'd seen a flash of bright, poppy red.

She looked through the glass wall of her office. Along the corridor outside, a woman wearing a circle skirt with giant poppies printed all around the hem was walking towards the canteen. Cherry watched the flicker of the red flowers swishing around the woman's legs until it vanished. She had a sudden vision of Doctor Poppy, peering over her gold reading glasses in her characteristic way and saying, 'Are you going to let people carry on bullying you, Cherry?'

But Alan wasn't bullying her! He was more like a mentor to her. She knew that her programme couldn't have been successful without him.

'Earth to Cherry,' Alan said again, with a smile that didn't reach his eyes. His fingers drummed irritably on her desk.

'I'm sorry,' she murmured.

Cherry had been apologising for her distraction and lack of manners, but Alan interpreted her apology differently.

'Am I to understand that you have no

developments to report?'

Cherry felt miserable. The last thing she wanted to do was upset him!

'No, no,' she said hastily, and then her words faltered to a halt as the tangle in her mind tripped up her tongue.

Alan was staring at her face intently.

'I think I know where you're going with this. You won't talk until you get your dinner. You're holding me to my promise to take you to the Correspondent's Club, aren't you?'

'Only if you want to.'

'I'm very keen on the plan. We'll go out as soon as I'm free,' he said, but there was no pleasure in his voice, and certainly no enthusiasm on his face.

Cherry felt confused. The date had been Alan's idea. If he didn't fancy the idea of her company, then why had he suggested a date in the first place? She didn't want to go to the Correspondent's Club if he didn't want to take her.

'It doesn't matter if you're busy. Let's forget about it.'

His blue eyes flickered, but otherwise his expression never changed. She'd noticed at meetings that he was very much in control of his feelings. She wished he were easier to read, that he'd reveal more of himself to her. It was impossible to know what he was thinking as he spoke.

'It is true that we'll have to postpone our date.'

It had been too good to be true after all. She wasn't the kind of female that Alan would want to take to a glamorous media hang out like the Correspondent's Club. Whatever impulse had led him to suggest the date had obviously evaporated and life was back to normal. A black and bitter depression swept over Cherry. She'd so wanted to spend time with Alan.

'Don't frown at me, Cherry. I'm going to New York. You'll be delighted when you hear my motivation for going to the States. It's an excellent result for Pony Princesses. You know I told you that all the major stations US stations have purchased the format? Well, I have to go to New York tomorrow morning to discuss the merchandising. Isn't that a worthwhile reason for my journey?'

It was so thrilling that Cherry's insides turned to liquid sugar.

'Why, that's wonderful!'

Alan smiled. He leaned forward, closer to her, a smile in his blue eyes. He tapped her cheek with one finger.

'I knew you'd be pleased. It would be fabulous if I could drop a few trailers about our new format for the knitting show while I'm there. What approach did you go for?'

She opened her mouth to tell him all about her ideas for a format that would make her knitting show original and exciting, but at that very moment, the woman in the poppy-printed skirt walked back past the glass of the office wall again.

It was sheer coincidence. The woman had bought a cup of coffee to go and was returning to her desk. Only the most paranoid person in the world would assume that there was any meaning in such a simple event. Cherry feared for her sanity. The universe was not sending her messages.

And once again she was wool-gathering while Alan waited for an answer. He did not like being kept waiting. One preppy eyebrow shot upwards and his charming expression slipped.

'I'm beginning to think that you've nothing to report to me. This is a very disappointing, Cherry. You've had a whole two weeks to concentrate on your new ideas. I'd like to make you aware that your performance review is due this month, and to remind you of the consequences of the board having decided to make our pay performance related.'

Trevor, the IT wizard who kept everyone's systems up and running, popped up behind them. He was also a very active union official.

'Did I hear you reprimanding our Cherry for not working on her holiday, Alan?'

Alan's blue eyes flickered sideways at Trevor, and then he gave a thin smile.

'Cherry, I do apologise if my enthusiasm for your work led me to step out of line. But as you are aware, the quarterly development meeting is scheduled for next week. I'd very much like to be able to bring your new format to the table.'

Trevor lifted a hand to stop Alan.

'The girl's got more important things to think about. Before you do anything else, Cherry, you need to free up a bit of space on your computer system. I'm getting overload messages on the main system, and it's also telling me that it's your fault. I've told you before about going on holiday and letting your emails pile up.'

'Sorry, Trevor.'

Iqbal, a second IT wizard joined them.

'Hello, Cherry. You look well. Holidays must suit you. Hi Alan. Congratulations on Pony Princesses. I hear your show is the smash hit of the year.'

Alan looked delighted.

'Thank you,' he said.

Cherry waited for her boss to include her, but he said nothing. A cold chill slithered down her spine. Could her new friends be right? Could Alan be trying to cut her out?

A gadget beeped in Trevor's top pocket.

'Whoops, come on Iqbal, we gotta go. Empty that in-box today, Cherry, there's a love.'

She watched them leave, then looked at Alan.

'Trevor and Iqbal don't seem very aware of my involvement with Pony Princesses,' she said.

Alan flicked a speck of lint from his natty blue blazer sleeve.

'As if I would ever downplay your contribution to the show's success! You know IT geeks. They don't live in the real world.'

'Trevor and Iqbal are not geeks!'

She hesitated, trembling, but she knew that she had to stand up for herself.

'Alan, I think you should have told them that it was my format and our show.'

Alan's smile was warm, winning and infinitely seductive.

'I'm sorry that was remiss of me. I will certainly set the record straight should a similar situation arise.'

Cherry would have been satisfied, if the woman in the poppy skirt hadn't walked down the corridor for a third time. She remembered Poppy's advice and Harold's warning, and to her own astonishment she heard herself demanding, 'Alan, I'd like to see a copy of the Pony Princesses programme, please.'

'What do you need a copy for? It's your show. You have all the tapes on your computer.'

'I'd like to see the edited version. I'd like to see the finished programme with the credits on it.'

Alan's blue eyes flickered to one side before he replied.

'That might be a little difficult. I've

sent out so many discs to promote your show for you that I don't have one left for myself. I'll ask Vivien in editing to cut one for you.'

'When?'

If he tried to block her access to her own programme, then she would know that he was hiding something from her. But the smile that he gave her was utterly carefree.

'I'll ask her now, so that I don't forget to fulfil your request,' he promised, and he whipped out his phone and quickly fired off an email. 'I can see that the issue is resonating with you, Cherry, and the last thing I want is a rift in our relationship. There, I've sent the request and I've told Vivien to expedite it immediately.'

Cherry melted for the last time. How could she suspect Alan of any underhand behaviour when he was smiling at her so openly?

'Thank you, Alan. I know you'll be busy today getting ready to fly to America. I'll walk down and pick up the disc later today.'

Alan beamed at her, and the warmth of his smile blew away the last wisps of her suspicion.

'Cherry, I can always rely on you to understand my situation and lighten my load. I have to hurry up to HR now, and collect my tickets from Jodie, but I couldn't resist calling in to hear about your new format. No, don't say anything. You have made your stance perfectly clear. I'll hear all about your new show when I get back from my New York trip. I will take you for dinner, and in return you will give me all the details, exactly as we agreed.'

Cherry was now convinced that Alan wasn't trying to stop her from seeing the credits of Pony Princesses — look how open and helpful he'd been about getting her a copy of the disc. But there was one thing she was sure of: he no longer wanted to date her. He was making the proposed meal sound like payment rather than pleasure! He must have asked her out on a sudden impulse that had cooled off over the two weeks that she'd been away. She had no intention of forcing him to take her out! She wanted a man whose whole face lit up when he saw her, not one who wriggled like an eel. She would let him off the hook.

'Never mind about taking me for a meal when you get back. I know you're busy.'

But to her surprise he shook his head.

'Cherry, Cherry, Cherry, do you doubt me? Of course we're having our scheduled meal.'

He turned to the office and called out loud.

'Gemma, Emma, Sally, listen up, people! Cherry has promised to have dinner with me at the Correspondent's Club upon my return from New York.'

Three shocked faces turned towards them. Cherry saw six stunned eyes and three surprised mouths open wide. Alan turned back to her and smiled charmingly.

'There. Now you can't cancel our date.'

I must have been having a brain-storm, Cherry thought. He actually wants to go out with me!

'If only there was time now,' Alan murmured, his blue eyes sincere. 'I'm full of anticipation for our date. Maybe we could schedule a coffee or a lunch today in lieu? We can touch base, maybe chat about your new ideas.'

He slipped off the edge of Cherry's desk and she watched his elegant figure heading for the door. As usual, he turned back before leaving. His smile was only for Cherry.

'I'll have Cherish rearrange the restaurant booking.'

He looked so handsome that Cherry was filled with the urge to make his life easier. She called across the room to him.

'Lindsey has your tickets.'

His brows snapped together and he strode back to her desk.

'How do you know that, Sherlock?'

Cherry smiled happily. It was a joke they often shared together. Her boss was always impressed by the way she could find out information that would help him.

'It's perfectly simple, Watson. I called into Human Resources this morning. Jodie's on leave for a week, so Lindsey is taking care of things.'

His blue eyes scanned her face.

'And I hope Lindsey was able to facilitate the issue you were bringing forward?'

'No, I need to see Jodie.'

'The affair must be critical if only the boss can handle it.'

'It is. I'll tell you about it when you get back.'

'Cherry, if you have a problem, I'd rather you updated me now. It might be an issue I could help you with. Please, feel free to confide in me.'

'Thank you, Alan. I would appreciate your support, and it's a matter that concerns you. I've decided to challenge the decision not to send me to France.'

His blue eyes were horrified. 'But, the trade show is over! What do you hope to achieve by complaining? It's not like you to be vindictive, Cherry.'

'What about the next one? I'm not going to be left out of the trade shows ever again.'

Alan came closer and put a hand on her arm.

'I see. Cherry, this is an important matter that requires serious discussion. I want to support you. We had better schedule our meal for today and not leave it until my return.'

'We can't go out tonight. You don't have time if you're leaving for New York this evening.'

He smiled at her winningly.

'I want to talk with you about this issue, and I know how I could find a window. How about we go in your car and you drive me to the airport after dinner?'

8

It's a very odd feeling when a moment that you've fantasised about for over three years finally arrives! Cherry found it difficult to concentrate on work for the rest of that morning. The atmosphere in the office didn't help. Thanks to Alan's very public announcement that he was taking her out, Emma and Sally were so jealous that they didn't speak to her for the rest of the day.

Gemma, who was the nicest of her colleagues, reacted in a completely different way. She was thrilled for Cherry and insisted they go shopping at lunch time.

'One of those dresses in the window will do,' Cherry said, stopping in front of a famous low-price chain store.

Gemma was as keen on fashion rules as Moira the makeover lady.

'You can't wear ordinary chain store

clothes to the hottest restaurant in town!' she insisted. 'For one thing Alan Jenkins is taking you, and someday I'd love to hear how that came about, but you have to think about your career as well. You never know who could be sitting at the next table. You have to look sensational.'

She dragged Cherry into a much more select boutique, and they found a gorgeous frock in orange.

Back in the office, word about Cherry's date had gone around. Everyone was looking at her and whispering. She didn't like the weight of all those curious eyes, and Emma and Sally were still sulking and glaring at her with jealous eyes.

Cherry sat at her desk and decided to concentrate on keeping her promise to the IT expert. She began clearing her inbox. She soon realised that there were too many messages to actually be able to clear them; it was more a case of organising them into piles! Time slipped by as she sorted all her messages into folders marked urgent, reading and file.

At quarter to four, she suddenly realised that if she didn't go now for her programme disc, she'd miss Vivien, who was on her own with children so always left early to pick them up from school.

Cherry raced up to the technical department, stuck her head into the dark editing suite and made her request.

Vivien already had her coat on. She looked angry when she saw Cherry, but she paused to answer.

'Yeah, I got Alan's email, but I'm out of discs. There's a new delivery due tomorrow or the day after and I'll print off a copy of your programme then, if that's OK?'

Cherry looked at the banks and banks of equipment with all their glittering switches and dials. There must be thousands, if not millions of pounds worth of the latest equipment and it was useless without five pence worth of disc! She wanted to check those credits and put her mind to rest.

'Couldn't the copy be emailed to me or put on a flash pen? I know you're on your way out, Vivien, but perhaps Zak could do it?'

Vivien's assistant looked down at his feet and Vivien frowned before answering.

'We can't do that. You won't understand, but it's because the formats are incompatible and the file would need converting, which takes time, which Zak hasn't got. He's busy on a project for Professor Abse.'

'You can't keep the boss waiting,' Cherry agreed. 'I'll call back tomorrow.'

Cherry felt uneasy as she backed out and closed the door. She paused in the corridor, remembering the brief episode. Yes, there had been an odd atmosphere in that room. It couldn't have been anything to do with her, though. Her request had been simple and authorised by Alan. She'd probably picked a bad time.

As if to confirm her suspicions the

door banged open and Zak strode out.

'What's your problem?' Vivien's assistant was shouting back into the cave of the editing suite. 'I might not like what you're doing, but I didn't dob you in, did I?'

Zak looked thunderstruck when he saw that Cherry was still in the corridor. He flinched away from her as if she were a poisonous snake, then ducked his head down and scuttled off. She distinctly heard him say: 'Oh, man! My life is the pits!'

Cherry told herself that whatever row was going on in the editing suite was nothing to do with her, but she couldn't help feeling that a tense atmosphere haunted the television company that day. As she walked back to her office, she felt all the disadvantages of a glass-walled open-plan building. Normally Cherry was invisible as she went about her work. Today people looked up as she passed, and then turned to whisper and comment to their neighbours.

She felt horribly uncomfortable as she trudged down the corridor. She knew why people were watching her: it was because Alan Jenkins had asked her out, but knowing the reason was no comfort. She loathed the feeling that everyone was watching her. She couldn't imagine why anyone would want to be famous and deliberately draw attention to themselves.

To top everything, as Cherry walked past the administrative section, Cherish looked up from her desk, glared at Cherry and then burst into tears.

'Are you OK?' Cherry asked.

'Shut up and leave me alone,' Cherish screamed, springing from her seat and racing to women's washroom.

One of the secretaries scowled at Cherry.

'I'll go to her,' she said. 'You get back to your office.'

Cherry hesitated and then walked on. Poor Cherish had looked heartbroken. The girl had a history of getting involved with men who treated her badly, but her upset could be work related. She wondered about popping over to see Ann in the News Department, who always knew everything, but then she decided that it probably was boyfriend trouble, and so none of her business if Cherish didn't want her to get involved.

Back in the office, Cherry made everyone a drink, then took her new mug over to her desk and returned to the task of clearing the pile of work that had accumulated while she was away.

She couldn't help sighing as she waded through the piles of inter departmental memos and meeting minutes. They all looked mind-bogglingly boring. Perhaps because she'd had a break from routine, she could see clearly that none of the jobs on her desk were to do with her creative work. Cherry had always put in a sixty-hour-week so any creative work had to be done in her own time. She'd accepted her punishing schedule as the price that had to be paid for success. Now for the first time she considered a different option. Could Harold be right? Would it be better to work as a freelance?

Cherry grimaced at the still full in-box on her computer screen. She'd better think about Harold's ideas in her own time as well. She'd be lucky to even categorise this lot by midnight.

She began sorting through the piles of work again, filing, pruning, and making notes on her to-do list, taking the occasional sip of black tea — which she found delicious and refreshing and to taste satisfyingly of tea — as she worked. She was soon immersed in the departmental tasks, yet a little part of her mind was still considering the business-minded aristocrat's sugges-tion. What with thinking over Harold's advice and wading through the myriad of odd jobs that people seemed to think it was her responsibility to take care of, Cherry was so completely absorbed in her work that it took a hard tap on her shoulder to make her look up. Gemma stood next to her pointing at her watch.

'Cherry! It's a quarter to seven. I can't believe you're only giving yourself fifteen minutes to get ready for your date. You can't have forgotten that you're going out with the most eligible bachelor in Manchester! I'd book a whole day off to get ready if Alan Jenkins invited me to the Correspondent's Club.'

'I think he'll end up cancelling,' Cherry said.

'He won't,' Gemma insisted. 'He made such a point of it.'

'He won't have time to take me out. He's going to New York.'

'His plane doesn't leave until one o'clock this morning. You're wasting time! Go and get changed into that new dress, now!'

All the time she was changing into her new orange outfit and brushing her hair, Cherry was certain that she'd end up looking a fool for dressing up because she was expecting a message to say that Alan was too busy to take her out after all.

But when she went back to her office, she saw him at once through the glass wall. He was waiting for her. He was sitting in his favourite position on the corner of her desk. The floor around him was surrounded by matching luggage. He must have been home for it. And he'd found the time to shower and change into an evening shirt of dark silk.

Gemma opened the door of the office. She was wearing her coat because she was on her way home.

'He looks gorgeous! You lucky, lucky thing,' Gemma breathed, as Cherry went in to meet Alan.

Alan smiled when he saw Cherry.

'We're a few minutes behind schedule. We must hurry. How many of these bags can you carry? If you could take one more, we could save having to make a return trip. Well done. Not too heavy for you? Good . . . Where is your car positioned? Why ever do you park in a location so far away from the lift? . . . Oh, it's rather a small model. Do you think there's room for all my suitcases? ... Well, that's a surprise, you managed to fit them all in. It's a good thing that you're driving, Cherry. It'll save the expense of a taxi. The airport's not far out of your way, is it?'

The airport was actually ten miles in the opposite direction, but Cherry didn't mind that at all!

She'd never been to the Correspondent's Club before. Despite its name, it wasn't a club as such, but the high prices were enough to ensure that only a select few could frequent it. Modern in every respect, it was located on the top floor of an old factory. Cherry couldn't help sniffing as she walked in: the aroma of delicious food and even better wine wafted around the bar area where people waited to be seated.

'Just a soda water, please,' she told Alan.

She felt good in her orange dress. Gemma had been right to insist on a new outfit. You had to live up to such glamorous surroundings. A lot of the diners were beautifully dressed. Some people looked so bizarre that they had to be wearing the latest in hot fashions. Florals were clearly in vogue. At least six women were wearing flowing maxi-dresses covered in flowers. Those flowery prints look nice for summer, thought Cherry, I think I'll buy a long dress.

Quite a few people said hello to Alan, and she couldn't help noticing that the glances they gave her, as his companion, were admiring as well as curious. One man looked at her long and hard, and then came over to join them. He wasn't as smartly dressed as most people, and clearly cared nothing for fashion. He wore old corduroy trousers and a crumpled white cricket sweater, but intelligence shone from his kind face and he had jolly hazel eyes.

'Hello, Alan.'

'Hello,' Alan muttered.

Once again Cherry wished she could read more of what her boss was thinking. He didn't look entirely comfortable. Maybe it was the interest the man was showing in Cherry that Alan didn't like? The man was regarding her intently as he spoke to Alan.

'I hear that you and your latest equine TV success are the flavour of the moment, and I congratulate you. However, I have dragged my lazy bones towards you for the sole purpose of being introduced to your charming companion,' he said. And his friendly smile was aimed at Cherry rather than Alan. 'Do tell me her name and where you were lucky enough to meet her.'

Cherry thought Alan was wishing the man would go away, but he answered him.

'This is Cherry. She works in my office.'

The man beamed at Cherry and shook her hand warmly. He held her hand a little too long, but his touch was pleasant.

'I am Robin Cartwright.'

'Hi there,' Cherry replied.

Alan looked shocked by her casual greeting.

'Robin is the main executive at the BBC commission department.'

Cherry couldn't help being impressed by his important post, but Robin waved a hand and smiled.

'We are simply two strangers who are talking in a bar, but of course one always begins by talking about work. Are you an associate of Alan's?'

Cherry glanced at Alan. He seemed to understand that she wanted him to answer for her.

'I couldn't manage without Cherry.'

You could say that about a cleaner, thought Cherry. What an awkward situation. She wanted to remind Alan that he'd promised to mention her involvement with Pony Princesses, but she didn't want to embarrass her boss. The silence stretched out. Then she saw a crimson poppy motif on the badge on Robin's tie. When she saw the red flower, a shock ran down her spine. If Alan was supporting her, he wouldn't mind if she blew her own trumpet. Suddenly, she shrugged and went for broke.

'Pony Princesses is my format.'

Robin threw back his head and laughed out loud. He had a deep, low laugh with the rasp of a heavy smoker.

'I thought it was an anomalous concept to come out of Alan's head! My dear, you should have accompanied your programme to France. You should have been basking in your success. Pony Princesses was certainly the hit of the show. Everyone was talking about it. If you don't mind advice from someone who has been in the business for a long time, you mustn't let someone else take the credit for your work.'

'Alan isn't taking the credit. He promoted the show for me because it was so expensive to produce and I am completely unknown,' Cherry explained.

Robin's expression grew serious and he looked very hard at Alan. He didn't speak, but Alan shifted uneasily and Cherry was astonished to see Alan's cheeks flush bright red. She wanted to help him.

'My name's on the credits, isn't it, Alan.'

'Yes,' Alan replied, his tone very definite.

She wished she could understand the current of emotion that flowed between the two men. Robin raised his eyebrows.

'Her name is on the credits,' Alan insisted.

Robin's face was still serious.

'I'm glad to hear that.'

He held Alan's gaze for a long moment before turning to Cherry.

'Well, my dear, knowing Alan as I do, I have to suspect you were the sole creative genius behind that utterly delightful and very original programme. I'm always looking for talent. Why don't you bring your next format to me? I'll find you a place in my team if it's as good as Pony Princesses.'

He turned to Alan and gave him an unrepentant grin.

'Poaching, I know, but all's fair in love, war and television.'

Alan's brows snapped together in a scowl, but he remained silent.

A slim young man dressed all in black with astonishingly trendy hair shot over to them.

'Robin! Everyone's waiting for you. The table's ready.'

'Coming,' Robin said affably. 'Remember what I said, Cherry. There's a job waiting for you any time.'

The young man glanced at Alan before leaving.

'Alan, hello! Leaving us didn't hurt your career, I see. I thought you were round the bend when you quit the BBC, but your Pony Princesses programme is the hit of the year!'

The waiter came to fetch Alan and Cherry at that moment. They followed him to the table in silence. Cherry's thoughts were so engrossing that she found herself sitting and looking at the menu without truly knowing how she had got to her place.

'I can't decide,' she said, waving the enormous list of food away. 'May I have the tasting menu, please?'

'Awesome choice,' replied the waiter. 'You'll get the full benefit of the dining experience that way.'

Alan frowned over the menu for nearly ten minutes. Cherry looked around her while she waited and decided that she liked the modern decor. There was lots of pale wood and plenty of light which made the restaurant look very cheerful.

'Are you ready to order, Sir?'

'I'd better not risk anything exotic because I'm flying to New York tonight. I'll have a plain steak.'

'Awesome choice,' responded the waiter, which made Cherry smile.

Alan was moodily pushing his knife and fork around the white table cloth.

'I don't want wine, either. Just bring us soda water, will you?'

Then he sat silent until the drinks arrived.

'Alan,' Cherry said. 'I didn't know

that you used to work at the BBC.'

His blue eyes slide sideways.

'I'm sure I told you.'

'No, you never said a word.'

'There's nothing to say.'

'But it's exciting! A lot of people at our place would love to work at the BBC.'

Now Alan looked directly at her, and his blue gaze was stern.

'They might not find it as rewarding an experience career-wise as they antici-pated. I moved on because I wanted more freedom, and I had better warn you not to get too keyed up about any-thing Robin Cartwright might promise. I won't say he's an outright liar, but I will say that he's got a shocking memory and not as much clout as he thinks he has. You can't depend on him to pro-duce what he promises.'

'He didn't strike me as a show off, but there are a lot of people in television who promise more than they can deliver,' Cherry agreed. 'Thanks for the heads up.'

Alan was strangely quiet and she wondered what had upset him. Maybe he was preoccupied with his forthcoming business trip, but he wasn't even amused when her first course turned out to be ants.

'But they're still alive!' Cherry gasped.

'They are special ants from Sweden,' the waiter assured her.

She couldn't help laughing out loud.

'I'm not eating live ants no matter how special the little creatures may be. Do you want to try eating live ants, Alan?'

'Certainly not,' was his unamused reply.

Her next two courses were delicious and Alan's mood improved when a juicy steak was set before him. The poor man was probably starving, thought Cherry, no wonder he was quiet!

Her next course was a rack of lamb with the most mouth-watering herb sauce drizzled over it, and Alan finally smiled at her again.

'I enjoyed France,' he began. 'A number of people were impressed with my work and Frankie Fisher — I'm sure you know he's the chief executive officer of America's biggest channel — well, he said that he felt I was wasting my time working for a provincial company. He thinks I should move to a broader arena where my true potential can be showcased. He said that he had been waiting for me to devise a programme that showed my true flair. I felt it was good of him to take an interest in my career. He has so many demands on his time.'

Cherry found herself zoning out. Her food was delicious, but Alan reported every single important person that he'd met at the trade show, and every word they were supposed to have said to him! Perhaps she was tired, but she wasn't taking her usual interest in his affairs.

And yet, Cherry was happy. What fun it was to be at this sensational restaurant. The atmosphere was sweet with the smell of food and the air was full of industry chatter. She looked around and saw that a lot of talented and senior people who she knew by sight were in the room, drinking, eating, talking, laughing and generally having a good time.

Alan was detailing the number of times he'd had his photograph taken by the French press.

'That sounds interesting,' she said at intervals.

While she listened to her date with half an ear, she found herself people watching and wondering what the media crowd was talking about today. A funky-looking guy, who had to be younger than she was, caught her gaze and sauntered over to their table.

'Alan! Congratters on your hit.'

'Thank you,' Alan said, and he gestured at Cherry. 'It was my companion's format.'

The young man looked deeply impressed and handed Cherry his business card.

'I came over to meet you because I

thought you looked like a gorgeous woman. You're brilliant as well. How lucky is that?'

'Not lucky at all, for you!' snapped Alan, glaring at the young stud. 'Cherry's with me! Clear off!'

The young man's eyebrows shot up at Alan's tone. He shrugged.

'Nice meeting with you, Cherry. Call me sometime.'

Cherry watched the funky young man leave, and wished that Alan hadn't been so rude, but she couldn't help being thrilled by his manner as well. It was lovely that her boss had publicly given her credit for her programme, and he couldn't have made it more clear that they were a couple. All her doubts vanished like snow in the sunshine. She smiled at him warmly.

'Thanks for remembering what I said.'

He smiled back, caringly.

'You can trust me to foster your career. Won't you take my advice, Cherry and put the past behind you?

I'll make you a deal. You forget about making a fuss because you didn't go to the last trade show and I promise that one way or another, I'll get you to the next one.'

His blue eyes were startlingly intent. You could see that he really cared about her answer. He was waiting for her response.

Cherry nodded her head, thought-fully, 'Well,' she began.

Alan leaned forward and caught her hand, holding it openly on the table so that the whole world could see they were together.

'That's my girl,' he assured her, smiling. 'Onwards and upwards, that's the way.'

Cherry smiled back at him.

'You're right. It would be better to put my energy into the next show.'

Alan kept hold of her hand. Some-what to her own surprise, it was Cherry who took her hand away from his. It was very hot in the restaurant, which is probably why she wasn't enjoying the touch of his skin.

Life took a turn for the better when the pudding came. It was an extravagant concoction of spun sugar, fruit and ice cream set in a dish so lovely that she couldn't help exclaiming in pleasure.

'It's the Himalayan Snow Egg,' the waiter told her. We've never, ever, ever, been awarded less than five stars for this dish by anyone.'

Alan seemed to have talked himself into a good mood by the time his own vibrantly-coloured Snow Egg arrived.

'Now, darling,' he said, and Cherry nearly died when she saw how brilliantly his blue eyes were sparkling. 'Surely the time is right to give me a preview of your new show.'

'It's called Clickety Click,' Cherry told him, beaming at him.

'I like the title! Do you have a catch phrase?'

'Get your rhythm sticks moving!'

Alan beamed at her.

'You have a real talent for making dull things sound interesting.'

Cherry had begun to enthuse before his words sank in.

'I want my programme to be interactive. Members of the public can join in and . . .'

Then she suddenly felt as if someone had put an ice bucket on her head and freezing water was cascading over her head and down her spine.

'What did you say? Dull? Knitting's not dull! That's the whole point of my programme!'

'I do apologise,' Alan said. He leaned across the table and put one hand on Cherry's arm in a conciliatory gesture. 'That was an unfortunate remark. I actually don't know anything about knitting.' His face crinkled up in a smile. 'I'm a man! I can't help it. You said 'interactive'. I like the sound of interactivity. Management are keen on involving members of the community wherever possible. Please, carry on outlining the format for your pro-gramme.'

The moment's gone, Cherry thought,

a wave of exhaustion flowing over her. She looked at her watch.

'Alan, have you seen the time?'

He sprang to his feet.

'You can tell me more in the car. Quickly now, let's get out of here. How are you going to pay for your half of the bill?'

Too impatient to wait for the waiter, Alan grabbed Cherry's credit card and shot over to the bar to settle the bill. Cherry waited for him in the lobby.

The slim young man with astonishingly trendy hair who'd been sitting with Robin Cartwright stopped next to her and smiled.

'Hello. All alone? Be careful. Robin will kidnap you. He's determined to have you join our creative team.'

'He wasn't serious was he? I thought it was a line.'

'Robin never says anything that he doesn't mean. He's the real old-fashioned kind of gentleman. His word is his bond and all that. There are not many people like Robin working in television, more's the pity, but you can trust him.

'You can't hand out posts in the BBC to people you meet in restaurants,' Cherry protested.

'If you've got another format as good as your last one, there'll be a job waiting for you on the development team,' the young man insisted. 'You should check us out. We're a pretty friendly bunch.'

He lifted a hand in farewell and left her as Alan panted up.

'Hurry up, Cherry. I'll miss my plane.'

On the way to the airport Alan asked again about her new format, but Cherry was genuinely tired.

'The road is too busy. I can't talk and drive, Alan,' she protested.

'Oh well,' he grumbled. 'I suppose I'll have to make do with the few shreds of information you've seen fit to dole out. It's called Clickity Click and it's interactive. I suppose that's enough to start the sales process.'

She drove her little car up to the drop off point and got out to help Alan put his cases on a trolley. Of course he was flying first class.

'Will you make your flight?'

He checked his watch.

'With about thirty seconds to spare.'

His blue eyes bored into hers as he put a hand under her chin.

'This evening should have had more time allocated to talking about you. What a shame I have to go to the States. Do we have a date when I get back?'

Cherry's knees went weak and she nodded.

'Good! I'll look forward to hearing more about your format for Clickity Click. I'll drop a few teasers in New York. They're huge on interactivity, so they should love your concept of audience participation. Everyone will love it. When I get back, we'll wow them at the development meeting! Do you promise me to put a presentation together?'

He held her gaze for a long, electric second, until she nodded again. Then he pulled her closer and Cherry's knees trembled beneath her as she realised that he was going to kiss her.

'Excuse me,' said a woman in uniform. 'This is the quick drop off point. If you don't mind, fond farewells have to be said in the short-stay car park.'

Alan released his hold on Cherry.

'I must go,' he said, with another glance at his watch.

The automatic glass doors shot open and both Cherry and the woman in uniform watched him striding towards the first class check-in desk.

'Well isn't he every woman's dream?' sighed the traffic warden. 'Will he be away long?'

'Only a week, and we have a date when he gets back,' Cherry told her, and she drove home in a daze, feeling like the luckiest woman in the world.

9

The next morning, Cherry knew that she should carry on instilling some kind of order to her desk, but how much more fun it would be to create a stunning presentation for her new programme, Clickity Click. A slick presentation was important because image was everything in this business, and she had to make the format look good if she were to sell the idea of a knitting show to the development team. It was justifiable because Alan was her boss and he'd told her to spend time on it.

She opened a blank file and looked at the empty white page.

Gemma strode into the office and made a beeline for Cherry's desk, her face full of curiosity.

'Well?' she demanded.

'You were right about the dress,'

Cherry told her. 'Thank you. I'd have felt completely out of place in my every-day clothes.'

Gemma pulled a chair next to Cherry and turned eager blue eyes on her.

'I am not interested in the dress. Tell me everything!'

'I had a fabulous time,' Cherry admitted.

She described the restaurant, the food, the decor, the people she'd seen and the people she'd met.

'You are lucky! Fancy you getting to meet Robin Cartwright. He's very well thought of. I've never met anyone with a bad word to say about him. How unusual is that?'

'Did you know Alan used to work with him at the BBC?'

Gemma leaned forward confidentially.

'Nobody mentions it. I've heard that the Beeb told Alan that he had to put his notice in or they would sack him.'

'No! That can't be right.'

'It does seem odd,' Gemma agreed.

'It's probably not true, but the story goes that our Alan was caught in a fiddle of some kind.'

'I do not want to listen!'

'Hey, it was just between us two, and you did ask me. Let's change the subject. What did you and Alan talk about?'

A vision of Alan droning on about himself popped into Cherry's mind. He hadn't been at his best of course, anyone would be distracted if they were about to fly to America, but she was shocked by the reaction Gemma's question provoked. The secret truth was that she had found Alan's conversation dull rather than scintillating. Maybe she should have worked harder to change his mood.

'We talked about television matters mostly,' Cherry said with perfect truthfulness.

'Did he kiss you?'

'There wasn't time,' Cherry sighed.

The phone shrilled urgently and Gemma went back to her own desk, leaving Cherry to think over their conversation.

She didn't believe for one moment that Alan had been sacked from the BBC. Look how friendly his ex-colleagues had been. The young man with the trendy hair had said, 'I thought you were round the bend to leave us'. That wasn't how people talked to someone who'd left the company in disgrace. She was certain that the story was a vicious rumour.

She wished that she could feel as certain that her long-held image of Alan was accurate. What should have been the most exciting date of her life had been a let-down. But what had spoiled it, Alan himself or the suspicion that her new friends had planted in her mind?

She was sure they were wrong about Alan exploiting her. Yes, she was absolutely sure they were wrong. Yet she felt uncomfortable about the way Alan had said, 'We'll wow them at the development meeting'. She wasn't stupid! She didn't seem to be getting a lot of 'we' so far as Pony Princesses was concerned. Everyone she'd spoken to since the format had become a success had had to be told that she was involved. Nobody seemed to be aware that she'd come up with the original concept and the format.

Yet once she'd told Alan that being credited was important to her, look how quick he'd been to tell people it was her format. Her friends had to be wrong and one way to prove it was to check that she had full and proper credit on the official version of her programme.

She picked up her phone and rang the editing suite.

'Zak speaking.'

'It's Cherry. When would it be convenient for me to collect the copy of my programme?'

'Viven's not here.'

'Couldn't you put a copy on a disc for me?'

'Sorry, mate. Viven told me not to. That is, she wants to do it herself.'

'Do you know when she's planning to make my copy?'

'Never, no, I mean in a few days. She'll do it when the discs come. She said that I had to say that they hadn't arrived, like.'

'Please tell her that I'll call tomorrow.'

Cherry sat thinking for a long moment, looking at the blank page on her computer screen. Up until this very second, she'd done no work on her new programme in company time. It was hers alone.

It was ridiculous to suspect Vivien of conspiring with Alan to withhold a copy of the finished programme, and yet she felt uneasy. Was she being stalled?

Harold's face floated into her mind and his advice rang in her ears. 'At least promise me that you'll wait and see what this boss of yours has done with your last programme before you make him a present of your new one.'

She thought of Alan, so handsome and smiling and utterly desirable. How wonderful he'd looked striding into the airport, and he'd promised her a date when he got back from New York. For three long years she'd suffered from unrequited love, and now she was finally dating the man of her dreams. Was she crazy to allow her dreams to be not just influenced but ruined by the suspicions of people who'd never even met Alan and who knew nothing about television?

Yet Harold seemed to have her best interests at heart. He'd texted her that morning with the number of a good lawyer. He advised her to get in touch at once, promising that Tagtar Natoa represented a number of people who worked in the world of media. The lawyer understood royalties and broadcasting rights, and he would also help Cherry challenge her employer's decision not to allow her to represent the company.

She turned back to her blank screen. She believed in Alan, but he himself was always saying that in business you had to keep your cards to your chest and not play them until the time was right. It wouldn't hurt to be cautious. She closed down the presentation programme and dialled the lawyer's number.

He sounded very pleasant and pleased to hear from Cherry.

'I can assure you that any friend of Harold's gets my premier services,' he said.

'Did you go to the same school as Harold?' Cherry asked.

'Yes. Why do you ask?'

'Because, Mr Natoa, you speak with the same accent. You sound exactly like Harold.'

'Yes, we all get an accent as well as a tie as a souvenir of our old school! Please, I'd like you to call me Tagtar, I'm sure we're going to be friends. If you can forgive me for what I'm about to say next, that is. Do you think you can wait a week for your first appointment? I'm off to St Bart's tomorrow to work on my tan.'

They agreed on a date. Cherry scribbled the appointment into her diary and entered it into her computer as well. It's going to be a busy week, next week, she thought. I'd better get my head down and clear this backlog while I've got a quiet moment.

At that very moment, the phone shrilled. She could have let it go to the answer machine, but then she shrugged and picked it up.

'Hello, Cherry. It's Teddy.'

When she heard his deep voice, a shock ran over her whole body.

'I hope you don't mind my ringing you,' he was saying. 'I want to ask a favour on Angelina's behalf.'

'Angelina?' Cherry echoed, feeling quite dazed by the call. She hadn't expected to hear Teddy's voice.

His friendly chuckle sounded so familiar. It brought back recollections of her time in the spa. Memories of the freshness of Blackpool's sunny beach seemed to fill the room.

Teddy said, 'Have you heard from Angelina?'

'I've only had a few short emails. She

told me that she was seeing Harold.'

Teddy's deep, open laugh was so attractive.

'I think we'd have to accuse Angelina of understating the case. It's a gigantic romance on both sides! Harold's taken her to all his treasured places, including to Wimbledon to watch the tennis, Ascot to have a flutter on the horses and to dinner at his old college in Oxford. In return she's taken him to the greyhound racing, for a pie and pea supper and to the karaoke version of Mamma Mia where she made him sing along. They both say they've never had such a joyful time in their lives. I think it's true love.'

'That's lovely for them.'

'It is, but there's a problem, which is why I'm ringing you. Harold is serious about Angelina. He's met her parents, but it's not going to be easy the other way around. He knows it's going to be sticky introducing her to his parents. He wants me along for moral support, and Angelina would like you to be there for some female company.'

Cherry took a moment to consider the idea. Teddy gave her time to think before speaking again.

'Cherry, I said that I'd call you about the weekend because I want to assure you that I won't embarrass you. We'll keep things on a strictly friendly basis.'

She felt herself relaxing. He was so good at handling awkward situations.

'Thank you. Then I'll go if Angelina wants me to. I can understand why she wants support. Didn't you say that Harold's father is a duke? I'm feeling intimidated myself. Won't it be frightfully grand? What on earth would I wear at a duke's house?'

'You'll only need ordinary clothes for an ordinary weekend in the country. If the duchess is running true to form, the house will be crawling with debutantes that she thinks Harold should marry, but apart from that, it will just be the family.'

'That's a relief!'

'You said that you liked horses, didn't

you? You could bring riding kit if you think you might enjoy a ride.'

Cherry loved the idea. It was ages since she'd been on a horse.

'I'm starting to look forward to the visit. It'll be lovely to see Harold and Angelina again.'

Teddy gave his deep growly laugh.

'You'll see them, but don't expect them to notice you. They are completely absorbed in each other!'

'Just as it should be,' Cherry answered. 'I think young love is charming, and of course I'll help. Where is Harold's house?

'It's in Cumbria. Do you know the area around the Solway Coast?'

'I've never spent much time there, but I know that it's very pretty.'

'The countryside is stunning. You'll enjoy exploring it.'

'What's Harold's house called? If you've got the postcode, I can put in my sat nav.'

Teddy laughed again. It was such a friendly sound that Cherry found herself smiling too. There was something so lively about Teddy. Some of his energy seemed to be pouring down the telephone as he spoke.

'I suppose castles must have postcodes, but I've no idea what Harold's is. You won't need your sat nav. Harrington Castle is a huge tourist attraction. All you do is follow the zillions of brown tourist signs that adorn every road for miles around. You can't miss it.'

'You don't know me. I can get lost in a supermarket.'

'I'd be happy to drive you to the castle. I could pick you up at work on Friday, or your house, whichever is best for you.'

Well, she'd walked into that one, and, in truth, it would be lovely to be wafted up north in the lap of luxury.

'Thank you. If it's no trouble, I'd like that. You could collect me at work, if you really don't mind.'

'I wouldn't have suggested giving you a lift if I'd minded!' he pointed out, chuckling. 'Your office is in Media City, isn't it?'

'With a huge illuminated sign on top of the building saying Prize Televison,' Cherry said, laughing. 'You can't miss it.'

'What time shall I collect you on Friday? If you could get away early we could go for a ride or a swim before dinner.'

Cherry glanced at her still chaotic desk.

'I couldn't possibly get away before six or even seven. I don't mind driving myself up if that's too late for you.'

'Let's say six o'clock. I'll bring my tablet — it's full of those books that you recommended, so I can read if you have an urgent task to complete and can't get away until seven.'

Cherry felt herself smiling as she rang off. How nice Teddy was to talk to. How easy he made life. And it was like him to want to help Angelina and Harold. He had such a kind heart. Instead of getting back to work, she looked up Harrington Castle on the internet. There was an old castle, but it was a crumbling ruin and the family lived in a fabulous Elizabethan house set in beautiful grounds. She found herself on a real high whenever she thought of her forthcoming weekend visit.

She had so much faith that the travel arrangements would run as planned because Teddy was in charge of them, that it was a real shock when the receptionist buzzed her at four o'clock on Friday afternoon.

'There's a man and a whole load of parcels in reception for you. It's a Mr Cameron. He says you're expecting him.'

'Not for another two hours,' Cherry muttered.

She wondered what had gone wrong as she got to her feet. Secretly she was rather glad to have an excuse to put down the spreadsheet she had been poring over. She knew everyone had to do six jobs these days, but although she supposed someone had to check the budget, and the general consensus seemed to be that it was her job, she had no interest in how much the department spent on stationery every month!

The reception area seemed to be very full of Teddy. It looked as if he was not just keeping up on his new style, but improving on it as well. He was wearing a blue check shirt with navy blue cords and his scarf was tied at just the right angle. His hair looked great, too. It had been cut again, so he was obviously going to keep it short and styled. His face lit up when he saw her and his brown eyes filled with joy. She couldn't help smiling back, and she tried not to sound as if she were challenging the change in plan.

'Teddy, I wasn't expecting you for a couple more hours. Has something changed?'

'You could say that,' he replied, gesturing to the brown leather sofa behind him. 'I had to make a detour on the way here.'

The sofa, the floor around Teddy and two of the chairs behind him were piled high with enormous shiny purple carrier bags. Every single bag was a particularly intense shade of violet and bore the logo of Manchester's most famous and upmarket department store, Inglewhite's.

'Nice day shopping?' Cherry asked. 'I think you bought out the store. What have you got in all those bags?'

Teddy's cheeks flushed pink and his brown eyes held a distinctly worried expression.

'I am sorry. I know I told you that the weekend was an informal family affair, and it still is, mostly, but Saturday night has suddenly become a formal dinner.'

Cherry winced.

'I know,' Teddy said. 'I'm not looking forward to it, either. But Harold's dad is connected to the diplomatic service. He used to work for them in fact, and although he's now sits in the House of Lords, he's still got his finger in a fair number of diplomatic pies. Don't ask me what's it's all about, but apparently a Spanish archduke has suddenly agreed to visit on Saturday in order to discuss an agreement that the grandee has been refusing to sign for years, so it's white-ties and tiaras for all of us, I'm afraid and no arguing.'

'Couldn't we go another weekend?'

'Harold won't hear of it. I think he half suspects his parents of trying to delay Angelina's visit, and he's refusing to change the date.'

Teddy looked at Cherry with anxious brown eyes.

'I know it's a hideous prospect, but Harold says please will you not be put off by the formal banquet and come to the castle? And think about Angelina. She is going to need support more than ever.'

'Yes, but how can I attend a state occasion? This may come as a surprise, but I don't happen to have a tiara about my person.'

Teddy gestured to the stack of gleaming violet carrier bags that surrounded him.

'Harold didn't want to put either of you to any trouble, and he knew Angelina wouldn't accept a dress from him if he didn't buy you one, so the long and short of it is that I am the bearer of a new evening gown and a tiara for each of you. I hope you like them, and will accept them with the future Duke of Harrington's compliments.'

While Teddy was speaking, the chief executive of the television company, Professor Penelope Abse, was zipping through reception at her usual speed. The CEO was one of those frighteningly intelligent women who seem to sail through life more easily than mere mortals. Not only did she run Prize Television, she had a chair at the university. Her subject was communications. She was usually in a hurry, and Cherry had never exchanged more than a few words with her, but when the professor's glance fell on the enticing stack of violet packages, she screeched to a halt and looked at Teddy with a smile in her dark eyes.

'Did I hear you mention the Duke of Harrington? Isn't he negotiating the Spanish Stone Treaty?

'I've no idea,' Teddy said cheerfully, giving the professor his open smile. 'He's usually up to his ears in some diplomatic deal or other, but it's not my area of interest.'

Penelope Abse's gaze returned to the shopping.

'These packages certainly look more intriguing than politics. Are all these for Cherry?'

'Half of the bags are for Cherry. The other half are for our friend Angelina.'

Teddy turned and grinned at Cherry.

'I've come early so you can try on your dress and we can change it if need be. And, I know it's another favour, but could you have a look at Angelina's dress and let me know what you think of it?'

'I can't say what Angelina would like! Especially not for such an important occasion! Couldn't we send the clothes to her or couldn't she come here and try them on? I'd be terrified of choosing the wrong outfit for her.'

Teddy grimaced.

'The possibility worries me!' he admitted. 'But she can't get away. She's in Liverpool. Harold's picking her up tonight, but she won't be free until after the shops have closed. She's stuck with our choice.'

Cherry looked at Teddy in amazement.

'Did you say, 'Our choice'? Tell me you went to Inglewhite's?'

Teddy laughed out loud.

'Yes, but I'm just the delivery boy. Harold called Moira the make-over lady and asked her if she could help, and of course she had a brilliant solution. It so happens that her sister works at the Manchester branch of Inglewhite's as a personal shopper. Moira emailed her with measurements and colours, and the sister packed up an outfit for each of you.'

'What a pity,' Penelope laughed,

looking up at Teddy's masculine figure with open approval. 'I'd love to have seen a large and alpha male like you let loose in the evening gown department.'

Cherry was astonished when she realised that the chief executive was still standing in reception taking an interest in their conversation, and she was even more astonished when the woman gestured towards the carrier bags.

'Which of the dresses is Cherry's?'

'Let me get this right,' Teddy said. 'There's a system. The bags are colour-coded. We put green ribbon on the handles of the bags with Cherry's clothes in them, and yellow ribbon on Angelina's.

Penelope Abse picked up a gleaming purple carrier bag with a little twist of green ribbon around the handle.

'Come on, Cherry,' she ordered. 'Let's have a fashion show.'

Had the chief executive gone mad?

'But I'm busy, and you must be even busier!' Cherry objected.

Professor Abse smiled, and tilted the

carrier bag so that Cherry could see the package inside.

'Have you seen the label on this gold dress bag? I'd have to be dead before I could resist a close look at one of Nathan Wong's dresses! He's only my favourite designer. You have to try on this dress, and I have got to see you wear it. Come on!'

Cherry had never heard of Nathan Wong, but she didn't like to say so. Teddy pressed what seemed like a dozen green-ribboned carrier bags towards her, and she obediently followed behind the professor down the corridor to the women's washroom.

Penelope Abse sighed in pure bliss as she pulled out the first package.

'I adore clothes,' she confided. 'I can't tell you how close I came to taking my doctorate in textiles rather than in the considerably drier subject of the implications of the rise of social media for television companies! I decided to stick with media because I realised that if I earned a large enough salary, I would be able to wear haute couture rather than spending all day studying it in a museum, but I don't often get my hands on a garment quite as luxurious as this one! Open the bag! Let me see the dress!'

Penelope offered the dress bag to Cherry, who shook her head.

'No. Go ahead. You open it.'

Cherry watched as the professor reverently slid down the zip and exposed a froth of deep dusky pink inside.

'Oh, it's pink!' she breathed.

'It's all different shades. I love pink!'

They smiled at one another in excitement. Cherry had never imagined such a chummy scene, but here she was, being all girly over clothes with the chief executive of Prize Television!

'Oh, Cherry!' breathed Penelope. 'Look at this! It's made of linen rather than an evening fabric. That's so unusual, but it works! A boned bodice! Layers of dip-dyed pink! Oh, and it's all hand finished! This dress is an absolute marvel!'

She flipped open the foaming layers of the pink skirt so the underside showed and began examining the seams.

'Is there anything more adorable than parcels and tissue paper and haute couture?' she said, flipping the dress back and turning her attention to the pleats and folds of the bodice. 'Hmm, cut on the bias. Goodness, there's a snowstorm of notes tucked in with the dress.'

Cherry took the envelopes. There was a formal invitation for the weekend from Harold. There was also a hand written note from him, thanking her for coming to support Angelina. There was a note from Angelina herself, apologising for have been too wrapped up in Harold to have been in touch and begging Cherry to forgive her and saying that she must come to the castle because she couldn't face the weekend without her. There was a print out from Moira, assuring Cherry that no personal information had been divulged to

Harold or to Teddy and that her sister could be trusted to keep any information Moira had sent her completely private. There was a print of an email from someone called Olive, who turned out to be Moira's sister, the personal shopper, hoping that her choice of clothes was okay and saying that that the shop was open until eight o'clock that evening if Cherry needed to change anything. And there was one more handwritten note from Harold, written after the first note, bewailing the change in plan, fervently thanking Cherry for her help and praying that she'd enjoy the frock.

Penelope had been waiting impatiently for Cherry to finish reading.

'Try on the dress,' she urged. 'I want to see it being worn.'

Cherry headed for a cubicle so that she could be private, but Penelope giggled.

'There's no way this enormous skirt will fit into a cubicle. You'll have to try it on out here.'

'I hope no one comes in,' Cherry said.

'Seeing this dress would brighten up anybody's day, but yes, they might get a surprise!'

They both laughed like teenagers.

Cherry couldn't help a frisson of excitement as she slipped out of her top garments and reached for the admittedly fabulous dress. It had more structure and personality than anything she'd ever worn. She looked in the mirror. She'd never worn such an incredible gown, yet she felt like herself in it.

'Clever,' said Penelope walking round Cherry and examining every detail of the evening gown with absorbed black eyes. 'I love Nathan Wong's cut, but what a good choice of dress for the situation. The pleating around the bodice expands and contracts as needed, which means that it fits you as if it were made for you. It's totally amazing, except for the fact that your bra straps are showing. You need a different bra under it. I'm surprised there isn't one sewn in already. No, that was silly of me. How could Nathan know what size the person who bought his dress would be?'

The chief executive began rummaging through the other violet bags.

'There's a choice of two bras in this one,' she said.

Cherry checked the size on the label on the skin-toned underwear.

'They'll fit me,' she said. 'I don't need to try them on.'

'I like this brand as well. Oh, how thoughtful. The shopper has put in a selection of matching underwear as well: a camisole, French knickers, ordinary knickers, a thong. What do you usually wear?'

Cherry felt her face growing hot with embarrassment. This was an intimate conversation to be having with the big boss!

'I'll wear whatever suits the dress. All the clothes are the right size. I don't need to try anything else on.'

'You have to try on the shoes!' Penelope said firmly. 'Look what I found! It's only an emerald box with real live shoes by Shelby Shoes inside! Oh, my word! Cinderella would die for these slippers.' She took them out of the tissue paper with reverence and held them out to Cherry. 'Try them on!'

The evening shoes were perfect and utterly delicious, if rather higher than Cherry would usually wear.

'I'll have to walk carefully in these heels,' she said, admiring the vertiginous heels, the thin straps of dusky pink leather and the sparkling crystals.

'I'm going to see this personal shopper tomorrow! She's a marvel,' cried Penelope, rummaging through the other carrier bags. 'Look, she's put in a second pair of shoes of the same colour and they are flat. You could wear these ballet slippers if the heels on the sandals are too high.'

The flat shoes were pretty, and made of the same luxurious leather as the high heels. They would be comfortable. Cherry looked down at the high, fashionable and perfectly made shoes she was wearing. She'd never seen her feet look so beautiful!

'I'll wear this pair,' she decided.

Penelope actually stroked the gorgeous shoes before she put them back in their box.

'It's such a gorgeous shade of dark pink. I think they call it Chinese Peony, and it's perfect on you. It makes your skin glow and your hazel eyes look full of colour. How did this personal shopper get all the colours so right for you? You've never met, have you?'

'No, but I had a make-over with her sister. Moira did a colour analysis in one of the sessions. She gave me a set of cards with all the colours she thinks I should wear. I expect her sister uses the same system.'

'I am so going to see those sisters,' Penelope said.

Cherry began to take off the designer

gown. The garment was so well-constructed and had such frothy skirts that it took both of the women to wrestle it back into the dress bag. Cherry was struck with shyness when they'd packed the tissue paper and the dress and the shoes and the underwear back into the all the carrier bags.

'I'd better get back to work,' she muttered.

'I don't think so. Not without trying on your tiara.'

Penelope held out another box. This one was dark blue with a gold crest stamped on the lid. Just the box looked as if it had been more expensive than every single piece of the costume jewellery that Cherry had ever owned.

'Those stones aren't real, are they?' she said faintly.

'I doubt if it will be made with precious gems, but I'd guess at quality crystals because it's from a good jewellers,' Penelope said.

Cherry reached for the box and then froze with her hand in midair.

'I can't! I truly can't wear a tiara. I'm not a tiara person!'

Penelope looked curious.

'Are you not? I was so excited about the clothes, that I never asked you why you were dining formally with the Duke of Harrington.'

'I'm only going to help a friend,' Cherry told her, explaining rapidly.

Penelope laughed at her with fun in her dark eyes and opened the box with decision.

'It won't kill you to wear a tiara for one night. Pretend you're on a hen night. Oh, look! It's so cute. It's the teeniest, tiniest tiara in captivity! It's sweet. Try it on.'

Cherry perched the glittering head-band over her blonde curls and surveyed the elegant rose and ruby gems.

'It's not too embarrassing,' she admitted, feeling relived.

Now that she'd seen everything, Penelope finally let Cherry go, but she walked back to the reception area with her chatting as if they were best friends.

'Can I have a look at your friend's outfit?'

'I'd be glad of your opinion.'

The receptionist and Gemma were chatting to Teddy, but he turned at once when he saw them. His stance was wary and his eyes were full of anxiety.

'Is it okay? Will the outfit do?'

Penelope gave him an enthusiastic thumbs-up.

'The dress is perfect and so are all the trimmings. I'm wild with envy. I want to see the other dress. Oh, my word! Is that a bag from Norris Kamli I see before me?'

After that, nobody could have stopped Penelope Abse from shaking out the contents of all the other violet carrier bags so that she could see the frock and all the accessories. Soon the reception area was a froth of tissue paper and designer gowns. Penelope held out a dark green dress made of flowing dark green silk.

'Wow, this design is sexy, and clever!

Look at the laces up the side. It is clever because it means that it can be adjusted to fit. It's utterly divine, but it makes far more of a statement than the dress they picked for you, Cherry. I'm not sure I could wear a dress that showed skin all the way down my sides. Do you think your friend will feel confident about a neckline that plunges like this one?'

Teddy's brown eyes turned to Cherry and when she saw the laugh in them she knew he was remembering the samba outfit that Angelina had been sporting when they first met her.

'I've seen her wear mini-skirts and low tops,' Cherry mused. 'And when you look at it carefully, there is plenty of fabric in the dress. I think she'll be comfortable with it.'

Teddy grinned.

'I'm glad you said that, because I can't wait to see the Duke of Harrington's face when he sees Angelina in that knock-out sexy dress.'

Gemma's head whipped round.

'Cherry! You didn't say you were

going to a duke's house this weekend! My goodness, how come your life is suddenly so exciting? What's your secret? I want to stay with aristocrats and go to the Correspondent's Club with Alan Jenkins.'

The brightness in Teddy's face dimmed at mention of Alan.

Now Penelope Abse turned her attention away from the construction of the amazing Kamli dress and she gave Cherry a sharp look.

'*You* went to the Correspondent's Club with Alan Jenkins?

Cherry rather resented the emphasis on the word 'you'. It wasn't a private club. Why shouldn't she go to a glamorous media hang out? She worked in media, didn't she?

'Yes, I did. We had a gorgeous time.'

Penelope's dark brows winged upward at the emphasis in Cherry's tone and Teddy looked frankly miserable. Too late Cherry realised that her emphasis had been taken for enthusiasm about the man, rather than the venue. She could have kicked herself for being so stupid. She'd misunderstood her boss and upset Teddy, but it was too late to retract her words now.

'I must get back to work,' Cherry said, rather feebly.

Teddy nodded. He still looked crushed. All the light had gone out of his eyes.

'If all the clothes seem to be okay I'll go and get a coffee until you are free. I only came early in case I needed time to go back to Inglewhite's for any reason. I know you said you couldn't leave before six or seven.'

Penelope Abse gave Cherry a shocked look.

'Good heavens! You can't keep this wonderful man hanging around waiting for you for hours. What are you working on?'

'I'm in the middle of the stationery accounts,' Cherry replied truthfully.

She then wished she'd said that she'd been immersed in something more vital because Penelope threw back her head and laughed.

'I'm sure that the stationery accounts will keep until Monday. Get yourself off to Harrington Castle, and Cherry . . . '

'Yes?'

The dark eyes sparkled.

'Be sure to enjoy every moment of wearing that wonderful dress!'

10

Teddy remained uncharacteristically subdued as he drove out of Manchester. The Friday evening traffic was diabolical, and Cherry was content to sit silently next to him and let him concentrate. He handled the powerful sports car with ease. He'd obviously got the hang of driving his new toy.

Having set off in silence it seemed easy to stay silent, even when they crossed the border into Cumbria and the roads grew a little quieter and the surroundings a lot greener.

As promised, as they drew nearer, every road they drove down sported a brown sign advertising the way to Harrington Castle, and Cherry half wished she'd driven herself to Harold's house. She would have been able to find it. Teddy slowed down and turned left between two massive stone pillars and swung up a steep Tarmac drive that led up a hill. Chestnut trees lined the single-track road and a herd of deer grazed beneath the shelter of several of the massive trees.

Then they breasted the hill and Cherry saw the house below her.

'Oh my giddy aunt!' she said faintly.

Teddy stopped the car turned so that she could drink in the scene. After a few moments he smiled at her.

'I'm used to the view, but a first glimpse of the house usually takes people's breath away.'

Cherry had looked up the estate on the internet. She knew that the original crumbling ancient castle was uninhabited now. She knew that Harold's great, great, great, great, great, great ancestor had built a house in the time of Queen Elizabeth the first and that the family had lived there ever since. She even knew that it had been built in the shape of a letter 'E' as a tribute to the queen. What she hadn't expected was the stunning impact of the lovely rose-brick and half-timbered building as it lay dreaming in the evening sun. The green of the parkland ran right up to the house, giving it a rural air. Its ornate patterned black and white walls and the many, many tiny widows seemed to be smiling at her. It had such a peaceful atmosphere. The house seemed to be curled up on the ground as comfortably as a sleeping cat.

'I'll show you round the grounds, if you like,' Teddy offered. 'There's a yew alley that leads into a maze; there's a pergola and a pagoda, and I'll try to remember which one is which. There's a mews and a dovecote, there's a fish pond and an apiary; there's a walled garden and a vegetable garden; and best of all there's a stables full of horses and a whole range of mountains to ride over should you get tired of the parkland.'

He started up the engine again and drove up to the front of the house. The building seemed to grow larger as they approached. However had they built such a huge house in Shakespeare's times without modern machinery? As they drew closer she saw that the perimeter of the house was flanked by old-fashioned pink roses and sweet-smelling rosemary and lavender bushes, and two enormous bay trees flanked the entrance to the building. It certainly wasn't built for approaching by car, but Cherry loved the way the narrow path ran up to the front steps and entrance. The Elizabethan manor exuded class and a sense of history from every pore and diamond-paned window.

Teddy drove the car around to the left of the house and swept into a cobbled quadrangle before another entrance. By modern standards the black oak door with its intricate carvings and arched stone lintels wasn't so very high and Cherry was glad that the duke's house didn't feel imposing,

'This is the west wing of the house, which the family use,' Teddy said, gesturing at the wall on the left. 'If you go around the corner you enter an identical quadrangle and you can see the east wing, which is open to the public.'

Cherry sat silently for a moment, soaking up the atmosphere of the house. The sky seemed very blue behind it and the evening sun was still warm. It was the most peaceful place she'd ever been to. She could smell flowers and cut grass. She could hear doves cooing. She could feel a sense of age and warmth and security flowing from the massive stone blocks that this side of the house was constructed from.

Cherry jumped out of the passenger seat and went to the boot to begin carrying her luggage into the house. Teddy shook his head at her.

'Let Tommy carry the bags into the house. It gives him something to do.'

'Good evening, Miss Hawthorn,' said a clear male voice.

She spun around. Firstly she was surprised to see a young, fit-looking man in a dark suit. Secondly she was surprised that Teddy had been so rude to an employee who couldn't answer back. Then she saw Teddy buffeting Tommy on the shoulder in a friendly manner and when Tommy returned the playful thump, she realised from their beaming smiles that they were old friends. Teddy turned to Cherry.

'Let me introduce you to the new breed of butler: background in the armed forces and managerial expertise. Tommy's your go-to man whatever the problem.'

Cherry smiled up at him. His light blue eyes were very direct. He seemed to be examining her thoroughly. She smiled.

'What branch of the service were you in?'

'The Queen's Lancashire Regiment. I served for five years.'

Tommy had brought a little trolley over to the car for the luggage. Cherry was glad to see that Teddy had been joking. He was helping Tommy with the cases. She added the two dress bags and some shoeboxes to the pile. Then she looked at Tommy. You could tell that he was a capable man.

'The TV company I work for is making a documentary about butlers,' she mused. 'I found it fascinating. Aren't you tempted to find a post with a rich family somewhere like Dubai and earn an astronomical wage?'

Tommy's smile was friendly.

'I tried it for a while,' he told her. 'I worked in China for a couple of years, but I missed a decent pint of beer, and there was no one to play cricket with, so I came home.'

'That's the last of the luggage,' Teddy said, and the three of them began to walk towards the house.

★   ★   ★

The atmosphere at dinner that evening was tense, there was no other word to describe it. The duke, Harold's father, who looked just like him, was huddled at the top of the table like a heron waiting, without much expectation, for a fish. He exuded a kind of remote unhappiness, or was it boredom? Cherry couldn't decide, but anyway the atmosphere wasn't his fault. The venom emanated from the duchess. The blast of her disapproval was directed at Angelina. Harold, Cherry noticed, was sitting at an angle, as if he were trying to use his shoulder as a barrier between his mother and his chosen bride. When the duchess did look away from her son and Angelina and glanced across the table, Cherry got a cold stare that made her shiver and wish she was sitting nearer Teddy's friendly warmth, but he was on the other side of the table, surrounded by debutantes, and looking, it had to be said, incredibly smart in a dinner jacket. Yet again it struck her that Teddy was a surprisingly handsome and glamorous man. She wished that she could have met him before Alan asked her out and then she would have been free to go out with him, and they could have had fun together, instead of everything somehow getting spoiled and tangled.

Cherry gave a little sigh and looked around her. The dining room, like the rest of the house, was a marvel of black oak and decorated white plaster. The furniture was museum quality and historical portraits of Harold's ancestors looked down from the walls. The dinner table was exquisite. The inky expanse of the table top reflected glittering silver and flickering candle flames. Cherry would have felt like a character in a historical movie, if it hadn't been for the computer-controlled hostess trolley that Tommy rolled quietly into the room and plugged into a socket in a discreet corner.

There were far more women than men at the table, but after all, it was supposed to be an informal dinner, even if everyone was rather dressed up. Cherry was seated with a tall fair girl in blue silk, who stank of heavy perfume, on her left and a jolly-looking girl with dark curls and wearing crimson velvet on her right. The fair girl didn't even look at Cherry, but, as Tommy began handing around the wine for the first course, the dark girl smiled.

'We haven't met before, have we? My name is Dodie, silly I know. But I've been lumbered with my nickname since school and I suppose people can't be bothered to call me Theodora.'

'I'm Cherry Hawthorn.'

The dark head moved closer towards her confidentially.

'Don't take any notice of old frosty-faced Fenella. She never speaks to females. She sees us all as rivals for Harold.' Dodie looked around the women at the table and then back at Cherry with a laugh in her dark eyes. 'Which of course, we all are! I can tell you that for a fact, because I know them all, expect for the red-head, who I've never met before, and you. Do tell! Have you come a-hunting our eligible duke?'

'Not me,' Cherry told her. 'But you might find that Harold is doing a little hunting on his own account.'

Dodie looked across at Angelina.

'No! You can't mean . . . Well! I do believe you're right. Why, he can't take his eyes off her. And look at his face! He looks exactly like somebody hit him over the head with a sandbag, and that always means a man's in love. Gosh, won't the others be sick! She's jolly pretty. Who is she?'

'Her name's Angelina and she's just qualified as an accountant,' Cherry said.

Dodie looked at her with a mixture of amazement and amusement chasing across her face.

'She's a what?'

At that moment Angelina smiled up at Harold.

'I'm starving,' she announced cheerfully, in her characteristic way. 'I'm that hungry I could eat a cabbage with its coat on.'

Dodie began to laugh.

'This is priceless! We are in for fun this weekend! Just look at his mother's face! She spends her whole time fetching home the cream of the aristocracy for Harold's inspection, and he's only gone and fallen for a Liverpudlian bean counter.'

'Angelina is my friend,' Cherry said, a little stiffly.

The dark girl put a friendly hand on her arm.

'What gorgeous turquoise eyes! She looks lovely and just right for Harold. You can see she's full of go. She'll cheer him up, poor soul. He deserves it. Good luck to him.' Then Dodie heaved a deep sigh.

'I can't help feeling a little disappointed, and mummy's going to be devastated. Oh, I knew we'd never make a match, but, you know, quite unreasonably, I had this little hope that he'd change, or I'd change and a miracle would happen. I do so want a nice husband.'

Cherry couldn't help laughing.

'I think most women do, if we're honest,' she said. 'Could you tell me who everyone is?'

Dodie was a mine of information. As Tommy held out a silver platter for the duchess to help herself to the first course, the dark girl began whispering sharp character studies into Cherry's ear.

'Frosty-face, you know, and believe me when I say that she's not overburdened with brains. Do listen to her bellowing across the table at Harold. She hasn't a clue that she's wasting her efforts! She's the duchess's favourite because her mother was a princess. The tall blonde next to her is Sammie, the Samuelsons, you know. Their estates are to the west of us. They used to be juicy, back in the day, Victorian lightbulbs or coal mines or something of that ilk, but now they are all as poor as church mice. Sammie had no interest in Harold until he developed his positively astounding ability to rake in the loot, now she's desperate to land him. Next to her is Lucy Macdonald, her father went to school with the duke, or was it her mother? I can't remember, but it's one of those revolting stories where the parents make a match of it while the children are in the cradle.

'It's too bad of Primrose. Fancy her inviting five females and no men. What's Harold supposed to do with us all? He can only talk to one woman at a time. What are the rest of us supposed to do? Then there's you and Angelina, and nice as you are, you do add rather to the list of extra females. Oh, wait a minute, there's a man! I say, he's rather gorgeous now that I look at him! I don't know the hunk! Why don't I know him?'

'That's Edward Cameron,' Cherry said, feeling an odd reluctance to use his pet name.

'No! You don't mean the mad scientist! Well! He looks amazing! I've seen him scurrying about in the distance for years, of course, he and Harold have been inseparable since they were children. But what, oh what, has happened to the face fungus and the baggy cords? He's too divine. Are

257

you sure it's Edward Cameron?'

'Positive,' Cherry insisted.

'If only he had a title,' Dodie sighed.

Tommy had reached Angelina and was proffering his silver platter.

'What is this?' she enquired, eyeing with suspicion a heaped pile of flat brown curly meat bits.

'Fried pig's ears,' the butler replied.

Angelina squealed.

'Ew! Take them away! I don't eat the oinky bits!'

At the head of the table, the duchess's head shot up.

'Chef follows a nose-to-tail philosophy when it comes to preparing meat,' she said, in an icy tone that clearly declared battle.

Angelina shrank into herself and her cheeks flamed, but Harold joined the fray.

'No pig's ears for me, thank you, Tommy,' he announced firmly.

And now sides were taken all around. Fenella, Lucy and Sammie took ostentatiously large helpings of the pigs' ears, loudly exclaiming about how good they were. Teddy and Cherry refused them, and so did Dodie, and so, to everyone's surprise, did the duke. Cherry soon realised that he wasn't making a political statement, he was thinking of his stomach.

'I must say that I'd rather have a good steak,' he announced wistfully.

The duchess actually reached across and pinched his arm.

'Pig's ears are very much in fashion,' she snarled. 'Take a helping.'

'Being in fashion doesn't make offal taste any better,' Teddy pointed out cheerfully.

The duchess glared at him. 'I don't approve of your new manner, Edward,' she snapped.

Harold was smiling at his father, 'Don't eat them, if you don't fancy them,' he advised. 'They won't go to waste. We can feed them to the spaniels.'

'Well, that's what we always used to do,' agreed his father. 'Must say I was surprised when this chef fellow started fetching dog treats into the house . . . ouch!'

The furious duchess had pinched her husband's arm again. He fell silent, but his bottom lip stuck out and he pushed his pig's ears around his plate without eating them.

The duchess now called her son's name. She had a particularly clear voice. She enunciated every syllable in every word and said it loudly for good measure. You couldn't miss anything she said.

'I saw Hermione last week. She was asking after you. Do you remember how inseparable the pair of you were the year we stayed in the dear prince's summer palace in Petrograd?'

'Can't say as I do,' Harold said. 'It was cold, I do remember that, and I was bored. Beastly miserable place.'

'Oh, no, dear. You had a marvellous time, and you simply adored Hermione. She's looking incredibly well. Shall I invite her for the weekend?'

Harold rolled his eyes at the suggestion. Lucy, Fenella and Sammie had expressions that changed rapidly, and beside her, Cherry could feel vibrations which suggested Dodie was laughing.

'Priceless!' she gurgled. 'Look at the girls' faces. They don't want to disagree with Primrose, but they certainly don't want to encourage a fresh rival! Poor things. If only they knew the race was all over!'

As soon as they'd finished eating, the duchess gestured that all the women should follow her. Dodie rushed off and began whispering animatedly to Sammie. Angelina made a beeline for Cherry and hung onto her arm.

'You're a real mate, Cherry. I'd have died in there without you!'

'And Harold,' Cherry pointed out.

'And my nicotine patches,' Angelina said, holding out an arm spotted like a Dalmatian's. 'I don't even need them now, but I put three on for this weekend!'

Keeping their arms linked for comfort, they followed the other females down a wood-panelled corridor and into a room covered in bookshelves. It was like being in a museum. The books looked as old as the house, with crumbling leather spines and faded gold titles. You couldn't miss the incredibly ornate plastered ceiling. It was so low that Cherry ducked as she walked in, but it was an optical illusion. It looked low, but there was room for six-foot-six Tommy as he came rattling in with his computerised trolley, now full of tea and coffee.

Cherry took a cup of tea and sat cautiously on a teeny-tiny sofa that was more of a bench than a comfy seat. Angelina sat next to her and huddled close. Cherry was glad when Dodie, clutching a huge mug of black coffee, flung herself at a beautifully embroidered chair with spindly gold legs and dragged it over so that she could talk to them.

'So you're the future duchess!' she greeted Angelina. 'You've given me quite a problem, for marry I must. Now that Harold is off the marriage market, there isn't another eligible duke in England, but Mummy will be just as pleased if I take home a multi-multi billionaire, and here we are, with an adorable one in our midst! The only problem is that Sammie tells me he's taken.' She looked significantly at Cherry.

'Why are you looking at me? I don't know any ordinary millionaires,' Cherry protested. 'Let alone a multi-multi billionaire.'

'You know Edward Cameron, don't you?'

'Yes, but he's not a . . . '

'He is!' confirmed Angelina, and at the same time Dodie burst out:

'Oh yes he is! Sammie says he's one of the richest men in the country. She's never wrong about money, but she also says that he's crazy about you.'

'Me! Oh, I'm sure you're wrong about that.'

Angelina shook her auburn head. 'Cherry, I keep telling you! That man's bonkers about you and you're soft not to snap him up.'

'I'm dating Alan Jenkins! I can't go out with two men at once.'

Dodie's dark eyes were full of hope. 'You're not dating the marvellous Mr Cameron?'

'No, I mean we've been out together, but only as a foursome, you know that, Angelina. There's nothing serious between us.'

Dodie's dark eyes were so probing that Cherry remembered the kiss on the beach and felt her cheeks burning.

Angelina looked at the tell-tale blush and said, 'You may not think there's anything serious between you, but Teddy does!'

Dodie sighed. 'Well, if you have landed him, it's my own fault! There he was, right under my nose all this time, and I never gave him a thought. I suppose I didn't look at him properly. I mean, I always knew it was his inventions that made the money, Harold's always been clear about that, but . . . ' She heaved an enormous sigh. 'Gosh, I must be shallow, but honestly, he did used to look so different, and he behaved differently as well. He always had his nose stuck in a mathematics book, I don't think he's ever said so much as hello to me; yet did you see him this evening, chatting and charming the girls? What a transformation. I wonder what triggered it, and how he managed it?'

Cherry and Angelina exchanged a glance. They weren't about to give away Teddy's secrets. If he'd not made his stay at Doctor Poppy's Health Spa public, then they'd better not mention it.

Angelina's turquoise eyes were innocent. 'Who knows?'

'Cherry knows,' Dodie insisted.

'He did say that he was going to smarten up and start dating,' she said, truthfully.

The ancient library door creaked open and the men trooped in. Harold peered around anxiously, made straight for Angelina and took her into a corner well away from his mother. The two of them were instantly absorbed in a murmuring conversation.

'How sweet!' Dodie said, then she looked seriously at Cherry.

'And you're sure that you're not involved with Edward Cameron?'

'I am not,' Cherry said, shaking her head vigorously. And to cinch the matter she added, 'As I said, I'm seeing someone from work at the moment. He's in New York this week, but we have a date when he gets back.'

'Goodee!' Dodie cried.

The dark girl jumped to her feet and smoothed down her crimson dress.

'Wish me luck!' she whispered to Cherry, and then she headed straight for Teddy.

11

The moment Dodie left her Cherry realised that her feelings about Teddy were perhaps more complicated than she had thought. There was a nasty cold sensation around her heart as she watched him laughing and chatting with Dodie, and that was plain selfish, because wasn't she satisfied now that her dream had come true and Alan Jenkins was her boyfriend?

Nobody came to talk to her, or even looked as if they knew she were there, so Cherry drank her coffee, which was piping hot, absolutely delicious and probably far too strong for so late at night, and went to her beautiful museum-piece of a room, feeling like a lonely outsider.

It was a feeling that intensified throughout the next day. Nobody spoke to her at breakfast, and then the promised ride wasn't much fun because Dodie came with them. She looked beautiful on a horse and, although she was friendly towards Cherry, the dark girl spent the whole time charming Teddy. Cherry could see that he had no objection to being charmed, in fact he seemed to be enjoying it, and who could blame him? It was no fun for a man being shooed away like a fly! It was a wonder he'd hung about as long as he had.

He probably only fell for you because you were the first woman he met after his transformation, she told herself. Now he's realising that he's attractive and he's enjoying himself, and good luck to him. What kind of a person are you? Do you want him to be miserable? Why aren't you happy? Just look at this incredible parkland!

You'd think anyone would be happy cantering over sweet green turf and thundering under the high branches of spreading chestnut trees, but Cherry couldn't help feeling like a grouchy gooseberry as she watched the two figures ahead of her, riding so close that their knees nearly touched. Teddy turned round in the saddle — he rode very well and had perfect balance — and shouted back that the branches were high enough to ride under because the grazing deer and cattle kept them trimmed. I know, thought Cherry, waving happily but feeling slighted He'd obviously forgotten that she'd grown up in the country.

Later they clip-clopped at a more sedate pace down a lane bordered with stone walls sprouting ferns and foxgloves, and then to Cherry's surprise they came out onto a beach. The air felt fresh and she could hear birds all around them.

'We'll let the horses paddle, and then we must get back,' Teddy said. 'I know you girls can throw on your evening gowns, but it's going to take me forever to get into my penguin suit ready for tonight.'

Dodie smiled sweetly at Teddy.

'Couldn't we skip the formal stuff? I'd rather have a curry in my PJ's in front of the TV, wouldn't you?'

He grinned at her.

'To be honest, yes I would, but Cherry and I promised to be there to support Harold and Angelina, and I have a feeling they may need us tonight.'

He was right! The extra people that Tommy had hired for the evening to help wait on the table had just begun to hand out the second course when the grand dinner erupted into fireworks.

The table looked magnificent, and so did the diners, who were all in full formal dress and sparkling with orders and decorations. Teddy wasn't wearing any decorations, but he looked amazing in his white tie. Cherry wished she were seated next to him, or opposite him so that he could get the full effect of the designer evening gown and the pink tiara, which secretly she was getting a kick out of wearing. But Teddy was sitting where she couldn't see his face properly and unfortunately both the oily dark fellow on one side of her and the rather thuggish chap on the other side were both looking down their noses at her as if she were a black beetle. Cherry had a vague idea that there were rules about who talked to whom and on which side and in what order at such a formal dinner. She wished she'd looked up the etiquette on the internet, but she soon discovered that knowing the rules would have made no difference. The timid remarks she addressed to the man on her left and then to the man on her right were loftily ignored. To entertain herself, she looked around the table.

Angelina was seated in between the duke and the Spanish grandee, looking like a mermaid in the green gown with her auburn hair flowing over her shoulders. Cherry knew that the duchess would have arranged the seating, and she thought at first that it was an odd place to put Angelina, because she knew that the two men wanted to talk politics, but the three of them had fallen into a conversation that they all seemed to be finding engrossing. Angelina sparkled like an emerald between the two men, and they seemed to find what she was saying utterly fascinating. The duke looked like a different man: his eyes were happy and he was speaking in an animated fashion. Cherry wondered what on earth they could be discussing until she heard Angelina say, 'Knock, knock,' and realised the Liverpudlian was telling them jokes.

The duchess was watching the happy trio with mingled suspicion and amazement. When all three of them burst out laughing, her brows snapped together with fury. She wasn't dressed to advantage that evening. Perhaps in homage to her name, she was wearing a primrose-coloured evening gown, but the colour was too pale for her and the fabric was too flimsy. The fine silk did her sturdy figure and weather-beaten cheeks no favours, and it clashed with both the sash she was wearing and the chunky diamond tiara perched unbecomingly on her over-curled hair.

Watching the anger that darkened the duchess's features, Cherry suddenly suspected that the woman had expected the two men to find Angelina a nuisance and was furious to see them all getting on so well. Her suspicion deepened when the duchess turned to look at her son, who was beamingly fondly at Angelina, and leaned forward over the table.

'Harold!' she barked.

'Yes, mother?' he enquired politely, and then, as if he couldn't help himself, 'What do you think of Angelina? She's certainly won father and the archduke over, hasn't she?'

He spoke all in a rush, and you could hear his love for Angelina in every word.

His mother closed her eyes and kept them closed for a long moment, then she opened them wide.

'We were speaking of dear Hermione earlier. I'd like to invite her next weekend. I wouldn't be surprised if you were to fall for her.'

Harold's grey eyes turned the colour of storm clouds.

'Angelina might be surprised!'

His tone was light, so maybe his mother missed the grim look in his eyes. She made a gesture like someone swatting away a mosquito.

'My dear, do be serious. I'm speaking of a woman whom you may eventually marry.'

'And I am speaking of the woman who I have already told you that I am most definitely going to marry.'

'I don't think so, dear.'

'What do you mean, mother?'

'My dear, I try not to interfere, and I suppose young men have to have their, well, their dalliances, but the thought of you marrying that creature is ludicrous. In fact, I have to tell you, that I'm not altogether happy that you brought a person of that type to the family home.'

Harold stood up.

'Then I'll take her away.'

'There's no need to be melodramatic, dear. You can send her away quietly after dinner.'

So far, the exchange, although bitter, had been conducted in low tones, but heads turned as soon as Harold stood up.

'Mother, you seem determined to misunderstand, so let me put this as simply as I can. Angelina is the woman I intend to marry. We are as one. If she is not welcome here, then I am not welcome here.'

'Bravo!' Dodie cried, clapping her hands together so that her diamond bracelets caught the light of the chandeliers and sparkled. 'Go, Harold!'

Fenella whirled on her furiously.

'How can you encourage such peculiar behaviour? I think that vulgar woman hypnotised Harold. It's the only explanation.'

Harold ignored them all and stared purposefully at his mother.

'Will you make Angelina welcome?'

His mother stared back.

'I will not!'

'Then we are leaving,' Harold said simply.

'Sit down at once! Harold, how dare you make a scene at a formal event and in front of your father?'

From the shocked and stunned expression on the duchess's face, she had never expected her little boy to defy her, but it was clear that he was going to. Far from sitting down, he simply glanced at her angry face, shrugged, and stalked away from his seat and up the table towards Angelina. Every face at duchess's end of the table turned to watch him go. The waiting staff fell back in consternation, not knowing how to handle such a break in protocol. The three people at the duke's end of the table were the only ones who hadn't noticed the row. They were all shaking hands and kissing one another's cheeks now, and seemed very surprised to see Harold standing next to them. He held out a hand to Angelina.

'I'm sorry to disturb you, darling, but

I'm afraid we have to leave.'

The duke stood up.

'Good heavens! Is someone ill? Can I help at all?'

The Spanish grandee shot to his feet, put one hand on his sword and bowed to Angelina as she got to her feet.

'Whatever the problem, I am totally at your assistance.'

Harold spoke gravely. 'Thank you both, but there is no emergency. I am sorry to disturb your evening, Father, but my mother has asked me to remove my fiancée from the family home.'

The duke stood up and looked down the length of the table at his wife.

'Is this true?'

She remained seated and made a gesture with her head that indicated the other guests.

'Perhaps we could discuss this later?'

'Perhaps later my son will have gone!' the duke thundered. His angry words reverberated around the formal room. All along the long table, shocked faces turned towards him, but he was focused on his son, Harold, who had one arm around Angelina and was urging her away from the table.

There was no trace of the subdued and hen-pecked husband he'd appeared to be the day before as he glared at his wife. She seemed aghast, and also a little afraid of the fury she had roused, but she still opened her mouth.

'We cannot let him marry this person.'

'We cannot stop him, and what is more I have no desire to stop him.'

The duke turned and called after Harold's retreating figure. 'Harold, if you would have the goodness to bring your charming companion back to me.'

Harold turned at once, looking rather surprised. His father gestured to the couple to stand before him. The duke was an imposing figure, in full evening dress, with his decorations gleaming on the lapels. His face was stern and very serious as he looked at his son, also formally dressed, and Angelina, spar-kling in green crystals and the mermaid dress.

'My dear Angelina, you are very welcome in my house, not only as my son's choice of bride, but in your own right. I am deep in your debt, because I know very well that it is thanks to your tact, your wit and your wonderful way with figures that Juan Carlos and I have been able to come to such an amicable agreement over the Stone Treaty.'

The Spanish grandee nodded in approval.

The duke reached out and took one of Angelina's hands, and then he reached out and took one of Harold's hands, and then he joined the two young people's hands together, placing both of his own on top.

'Bless you, my children. You have my permission to marry.'

'Thank you, father.' Harold looked deeply moved.

Angelina's turquoise eyes sparkled with tears. The atmosphere was so solemn that it seemed to Cherry that the wedding could never be as binding as this moment. She felt a lump in her own throat.

The duke then turned around and spoke icily to his wife.

'I believe the Dower House is vacant.'

'Harsh!' muttered the man next to Cherry.

Everyone settled to their seats and forks chinked and the staff carried on serving, pretending to ignore the duchess who was staring into space with her tiara tipped on one side.

As soon as the women withdrew for coffee, Cherry caught Dodie and urged her over to one of the diamond-paned windows where they couldn't be over-heard. She kept her voice low.

'What's a dower house and why is the duchess so upset?'

Dodie whispered back, 'You know this house will go to Harold when his father dies, along with the title?'

'Yes.'

'Traditionally, when a new duke marries, his mother, the widow of the previous duke, goes to live in a special house called the dower house. All the big estates have them. Two women trying to queen it over the same house never works.'

'But the duke isn't dead!' Cherry objected, feeling bewildered. 'Why should the duchess move to the dower house?'

'He's telling her to knuckle under or move out.'

'I can't believe he means it. He seemed to be so under her thumb.'

'Don't be fooled by appearances. Maybe Primrose has been too much in the habit of getting her own way, but she's just had a sharp reminder who the real boss is.'

'It's cruel. How could she bear to leave this house?'

Dodie looked over to where the duchess and the Spanish noblewoman were sitting on gilt chairs. On the wall behind them, a beautiful tapestry gleamed with gold-embroidered prancing unicorns. The dark girl grinned.

'Primrose won't leave Harrington.

Look at her now, chatting with Pepita, as if nothing had happened. She'll wipe this evening out of her mind, and it won't be long before she'll be telling everyone that she found Angelina for Harold.'

12

Cherry felt as if she'd been away from her office for a million years when she walked in on Monday morning. With its modern design, its acres of glass and all its glowing computer screens, the television building was a sharp contrast to the ancient house she'd spent the weekend in. When they saw Cherry, Emma and Sally turned sulky faces away, so they obviously still weren't speaking to her, but Gemma flew over in a rush.

'How was your weekend at the castle?'

'Interesting,' Cherry said, but before she could add any more details Gemma looked her up and down.

'What's the matter with you? You seem to be limping.'

'We went horse riding on Saturday. I haven't been on a horse for years. I can hardly walk.'

The phone on Gemma's desk shrilled urgently. She headed for it, calling over her shoulder.

'I'm green with envy! Promise to have lunch with me.'

'I can't today.'

'Tomorrow then, so we can talk.'

Cherry promised and went to her own desk. Her sore muscles twanged and she couldn't help saying, 'Ouch!' as she sat down. As a little girl she'd spent all day on her pony, now, three hours on a horse had nearly killed her! To make matters worse, she hadn't even enjoyed the outing, any more than she'd enjoyed the weekend or the journey home. At least Dodie hadn't been in the car with them, but Teddy hadn't been like himself at all on the drive home. He'd been in a tremendously good mood, roaring with laughter at the least excuse, but he didn't look at her properly. She felt that the special bond between them had gone, and she missed it horribly.

She switched on her computer, but

just as it sprang to life, a flutter ran around the office. Through the glass walls, the natty figure of Alan Jenkins could be seen approaching. Cherry looked at his tall elegance and waited for her heart to bound, but she felt nothing.

Alan smiled charmingly and greeted the other girls with a fine display of white teeth, but he walked straight to Cherry's desk.

Why aren't you thrilled, she asked herself. Then she met Alan's blue eyes and she knew. There was no warmth in them, only self-consideration and calculated charm. She looked at his slim figure, his styled and highlighted hair, his even tan, his button-down shirt, the perfection of his Ivy League look, and none of it meant anything to her, because the man inside the image didn't light up when he saw her.

'Cherry, dear Cherry, I've got so much to tell you. I've been working hard in America on your behalf, but there's no time now. I have to make preparations if we are to shine at the departmental development meeting this afternoon. Did you progress the presentation on your knitting show?'

As it happened, Cherry had. It was a detail she'd probably keep to herself if she ever got around to telling Gemma about the weekend, but on Sunday morning immediately after breakfast she'd been glad to make the excuse to herself of having work to do and she'd stayed out of sight, putting together a proposal for the new format.

Beautiful as the Elizabethan house was, she didn't feel comfortable there. It was too grand, too formal. She had no idea what she'd say to the duke and duchess should she bump into them; Harold and Angelina were wrapped up in one another; and Teddy, well Teddy was getting on so well with Dodie that he didn't even notice when she crept back up to her room and huddled over her laptop inside the four-poster bed. It was odd to look up from the glowing modern screen to see curtains that had been hand-embroidered over three hundred years ago. She wondered who had designed and stitched the lavish flowers and fantastical animals that rioted over the fabric. Long ago, when their men got difficult, had women run away to their embroidery as she was now hiding behind the excuse of making the best possible graphics display for her presentation?

Her wimpish behaviour, however, did mean that she'd got a lot of work done!

'Yes, I did, but . . . '

'Excellent,' beamed Alan, cutting her off. 'I have a great many details to attend to before the meeting. I'll see you there, Cherry.'

He walked away. She watched until he got to the door, waiting for him to turn around and say his parting words.

'We're a dream team, Cherry.'

As she watched him walk away along the glass corridor, a woman coming the other way brushed past him. She was wearing a batik sarong dress which was printed with grey herons.

Cherry looked at the heron print dress. Herons reminded her of Harold, and the chat she'd had with him just before she'd left Harrington.

'I've only got a few minutes — you know how it is at the moment — but I wanted to ask if you'd found out what credit you'd been given for your last show?'

Cherry had confessed that she hadn't been able to see a copy of the finished programme, so Harold had repeated his warnings all over again and made her promise to meet with the show-business lawyer he'd found her, and to keep her new format private until she'd seen her credits and spoken with Human Resources.

Moving with as much determination as her saddle-sore muscles would allow, Cherry got up from her desk and went to the editing suite. Vivien did not look pleased to see her.

'The discs haven't arrived,' she muttered. 'You'll have to wait for that copy.'

'I can't wait any longer. I only want

to view the credits. I'll watch the programme here.'

Vivien wouldn't meet her eyes.

'I don't have time to find it for you,' the woman said, and she walked out rudely, hardly bothering to mutter that she had a meeting to go to.

A thunderstruck Cherry stared after her, and then she turned to examine the banks of dials, switches, computers and gadgets. Even if she could find the programme, she'd never work out how to play it. You needed a degree in electronics before daring to touch a single switch in this room.

And then a large office chair swung around. Zak, Vivien's assistant, was slouched so far down inside it that Cherry hadn't seen him. His face was white and tense, but determined.

'She'll kill me, but this is proper wrong. I'll run you the programme.'

Cherry watched the opening sequence of Pony Princesses with a thrill of pride. It did look attractive! And then the words: 'An Alan Jenkins Production' flashed up on the screen in large letters, and behind that screen, in tiny letters, scrolled the legend: 'additional material by Cherry Hawthorn.' And then the show started.

'Would you run that sequence again, please, Zak?' she asked.

Her voice was shaking. Zak cast her a hesitant look, then he shrugged and ran the fatal credits again.

'Thank you,' Cherry said. Then she looked at Zak.

'I can understand why Alan didn't want me to see this, but why was Vivien so secretive?'

'Vivien thinks that he's going to be her man and going be a father to her sprogs, and all that. She promised to help him, and she told me to butt out, but it's plain wrong, isn't it though? She's well delusional.'

For a moment Cherry felt furiously, murderously angry. She understood a lot now, including how stupid she had been. And with that understanding her anger died. How could she be angry with Vivien for falling into the same trap that she had? She got to her feet, wincing as she did so.

'Where are you going?' Zak asked in a nervous tone.

'Human Resources,' Cherry said.

'Are you going to make a stink?'

'Not for you,' she assured him.

★   ★   ★

Tagtar Natoa glowed with good health. Even in a conventional lawyer's suit, he seemed to have brought back some of the relaxation and freedom of the Caribbean beach where he'd been holidaying.

'I love the sun', he confided, leaning casually on the bar of the restaurant waiting area. 'My wife is like a vampire: she won't come out on the beach until the sun's gone.'

They were at yet another of the trendy new restaurants run by a TV chef which seemed to be springing up all around the North West of England.

'It smells good,' Tagtar said, sniffing

vigorously. 'Ah, excellent: here is our waiter to seat us. Are you all right, Cherry? You seem to be limping.'

She explained yet again that her muscles had been overwhelmed by three hours on a horse, and then she told him about the dramatic events of the weekend while the waiter brought the menus and they chose their food.

'Now,' Tagtar said, 'tell me about your work situation.'

All through lunch, which was delicious, the lawyer listened intently, inserting the occasional question, but mostly just listening with friendly, dark eyes. It wasn't until he was sure Cherry had told him every single detail that he ventured his opinion.

'Your boss is not only devious but clever as well.'

'I've been a complete idiot,' Cherry sighed.

'If he'd claimed that the original format was his, or if he'd left out any mention of your contribution to the format altogether, there might have been a slim chance, but as it is . . . '

'I know', Cherry said gloomily. 'The credits are true, but not true. He did produce the show, and, it might sound odd, but I'm still grateful to him for that. I wouldn't have been able to produce it. Pony Princesses was ridiculously expensive to make, I'm unknown and it's a new format. Alan fought hard to get it made. If only he'd credited me for the format.'

'Ah, credit!' the lawyer said, smiling as he tucked into his lobster dish. 'I could be telling you stories that would make your hair curl when it comes to fights about who gets the billing! Do you want my advice?'

'Yes please.'

'Forget it and move on. This man got your first programme made. Save all your energy for promoting your second programme.'

The lawyer's dark eyes studied her intently.

'It's hard, I know.'

Cherry looked up at him and sighed.

'I made too many mistakes.'

Tagtar picked up the copy of her employment contract which he'd asked Cherry to bring with her. It ran to twelve pages, but he read it through in five minutes, wincing theatrically as he did so.

'Putting your name to this mediaeval document without legal advice was not the best move. You didn't quite sign your soul away, but your employers have the right to pretty much everything else, including the intellectual copyright to all the work you do while you are employed by them. It ties my hands rather. Let's think of the future. We could renegotiate this contract, or you could simply leave. I know Harold has advised you to freelance, and I'd be happy to act as your legal agent.'

Cherry was surprised. She'd looked the lawyer up on the Internet and she knew he was highly regarded in the media world.

'Really? That's kind of you!'

Natoa's smile radiated sunshine.

'Pudding looks good! Here's my Lemon Delight. What are you having? Coconut and Lime Heaven! Oh, it looks first-rate. I wish I'd ordered that! No, no. You are kind, but keep your pudding. We'll have to come back next time we meet and then I can order it. The food's jolly good at this place, I'll give the chef that.'

Once they were settled with their sweets, he returned to the topic of business.

'Any friend of Harold's . . . seriously. You have yourself a good friend there, Cherry. He'd pull my ears off if I didn't do my best for you. Speaking of which, this matter of the boss swindling you out of the trip to the television festival, we might be able to do something there. You said your Human Resources department knew nothing about it?'

Cherry grimaced.

'They couldn't believe it when I told them the story! Jodie, the head of the HR department, she was furious. I think she was almost as angry with me for being such an idiot as she was with Alan! I should have known that she would have supported me.'

Tagtar poured them both a cup of coffee and then looked at Cherry and opened his arms wide. His eyes were smiling and appreciative.

'Please, never tell my wife that I said this, but you are beautiful! How could you believe that you were too ugly to represent your company? This is the aspect that puzzles me exceedingly.'

'It's too complicated to explain,' Cherry told him.

Images of the school bullies taunting her flashed into her mind, then she saw her old self, dressed in black, hunching and hiding away from people, and then Alan teasing her and pretending to console her. But to counteract the unhappy past came the newer pictures of the admiration in Teddy's eyes, her image in the mirror after seeing Moira the Makeover Lady and, of course, Doctor Poppy doling out wise counsel.

She looked up at the lawyer and smiled.

'It's all history and I've changed now. I don't care what happened at Prize Television. I'm going to leave them, and I am going to take up your kind offer, and Harold's of course. I'm going to be a freelance creator of television shows.'

The words came with immense decision, and Cherry felt a sense of freedom and exhilaration that surprised her. No more stationery budgets! She would be free to spend her time doing what she loved.

Her new lawyer looked at her and smiled.

'I think you have made a wise decision. Will you hand in your notice today?'

'Yes. And I'm going to be creative about it! I'm not going to sue Alan Jenkins, but I am going to have my revenge.'

13

This was only the fifth quarterly development meeting that Cherry had been to, and when she remembered how thrilled she had been to attend the first one, it seemed incredible that she was now happy that this would be her last!

'Are you limping, Cherry?' asked the finance manager.

She explained about horse riding at the weekend all over again as the other senior members of Prize Television filed in to the meeting room and took their seats around the birchwood table. They all seemed to know that she had been to Harrington Castle and attended a formal dinner, and she came in for some gentle teasing about tiaras. Perhaps the clothes-loving chief executive had been gossiping. Penelope Abse arrived last, taking the chair at the head of the table and opening the meeting with her usual speed and efficiency.

'We won't wait for Cherish. I shall take the minutes until she arrives,' she decided.

One of the early items on the agenda was the new knitting show.

All the executives began by congratulating Alan on the success of Pony Princesses, and even now, Cherry was thrilled to hear that the date of the first transmission of her show had been set for three weeks' time, and the media buzz around it was terrific.

Alan Jenkins was purring under their praise. Cherry watched his slim figure and wondered what on earth she had seen in the man. How had she fallen for such a lightweight? He seemed like nothing but a shell to her. Her gaze must have been cold. Alan caught her eye and spoke hastily.

'I must give credit where credit's due. A lot of the success of Pony Princesses is due to Cherry here.'

Cherry watched the approving nods around the table and couldn't help admiring Alan's mastery of being a complete weasel. In the past, she had heard the praise and been satisfied, but now she realised that Alan, despite his words, was not giving her proper credit. His comment could have been made about any assistant or underling, and the executives were nodding happily because he was being a supportive employer. She could see straight through him now. She couldn't help smiling to herself as Alan introduced the concept of a knitting show.

'Knitting? You can't be serious! I think success has gone to your head,' the head of entertainment said, and judging by the nods of agreement he was speaking for them all. 'Knitting is boring and old-fashioned. Nobody knits these days.'

Alan's lovely teeth showed and he smiled widely. Cherry noticed that his blue eyes were calculating and watchful.

'That's what I used to think,' he

told the assembled executives. Then he gestured to Cherry. 'But Cherry taught me differently. There has been a resurgence in the old crafts. New knitting shops are opening up every day. Did you know that one social knitting website has over five million members?'

'Five million?' said the finance manager, sitting up and opening his eyes in interest. 'That will attract our advertisers.'

Cherry was thinking that yet again, Alan was seeming to include her without giving her proper credit. He was good at his job, though. It hadn't taken him long to make everybody keen on the new format. A few more words, and everybody was panting to see the new show.

Alan smiled at Cherry.

'Would you mind setting up the presentation?'

She smiled back at him. Once again she was aware of his clever wording. Why, she could be his secretary.

'I'd be delighted to show the presentation.'

She picked up the little gadget that held the presentation she'd spent so long putting together, walked up to the interactive whiteboard that hung on one wall of the meeting room, and slotted it in, just as she had five meetings ago, when she had presented the proposed format for Pony Princesses. That time she'd been blissfully unaware of how Alan was slanting things so that she was reduced to the role of little helper. She hadn't noticed a thing back then, she'd been so thrilled to get a chance. She'd been so nervous standing up in front of everyone, so convinced that Alan was perfect, but now she was different, and Alan was in for a surprise.

Her presentation loaded quickly. It was the first time she'd seen the slide enlarged on a big screen, and even though she said it herself, it looked good. Of course, her own graphics would be improved by the professional television team, but, even in draft form, you could tell that her new format had something. As animated knitting needles clicked out a piece of knitting to the refrain of a catchy snatch of classical music, a murmur of appreciation ran around the room.

'Ah, Bach's Sheep May Safely Graze,' Penelope Abse murmured. 'Good choice of music for a knitting programme.'

'It's an excellent choice. Bach is in the public domain, so there will be no royalties to pay,' the finance manager said, smiling happily.

'Next slide, please Cherry,' Alan commanded.

Obediently, but secretly smiling to herself, she operated the infra-red remote that advanced the presentation to the next slide. Every eye was trained on the background that she had designed from fluffy wool shapes. When you looked at the pattern more closely, the blocks of light and dark made up a moorland landscape and Cherry hoped that she'd timed it right, because she wanted people to have time to register the fields and the trees before a couple of adorable sheep appeared, bearing a banner that proclaimed, 'An Alan Jenkins production.'

The other executives were not surprised at the wording but Alan's mouth fell open in shock. His head whipped around and he stared at Cherry with anxiety clear in his blue eyes. She beamed back at him. He was worried, but he wasn't scared, not yet. He seemed to be trying to gauge her expression. She smiled at him happily, and he relaxed a fraction and gave her a thumbs up. He was so sure of her! She clicked the next slide. This showed a dramatic black and white photograph of a Shetland Islander knitting. As the camera focussed in on the sweater in the woman's hands, colour flowed into the pattern, lighting up the centre of the image, but the background stayed dark, the knitting woman faded, and in small letters, the legend 'with additional material by Cherry Hawthorn' popped up on the screen.

Alan's tension had returned. He coughed nervously.

'Next slide, Cherry, please.'

'Of course,' she said, with her biggest smile yet, and she clicked the remote control.

An empty slide flashed up onto the board. After a few seconds, a stir ran around the room. People stared at the blank white board in puzzlement. Alan gawped at Cherry, his blue eyes trapped and horrified. She dropped her smile to show him that she was deadly serious and returned his gaze steadily. The silence drew out until someone spoke uneasily.

'Is this the right presentation?'

'No!' Alan said quickly. 'There's been a mistake. I do apologise. Cherry and I will leave at once and put everything right. We'll bring our presentation to the next development meeting, won't we Cherry?'

'There's no mistake,' she said, and she turned away from Alan to look at the executives seated around the table. Their watching eyes no longer scared her. 'The credits at the beginning of this presentation are exactly the same as the credits on Pony Princesses. The reason I used the same format is because the two programmes have been created in exactly the same way. The proportion of Alan's contribution and my own are identical. Once Alan has had his say, I'll reveal my additional material.'

Penelope Abse looked at Alan. There was a small delighted glow in her eyes.

'You created the credits for Pony Princesses, didn't you, Alan?'

'Well now, I'm not sure. I think the graphics people . . . '

'Oh no!' broke in the head of the art department shooting to her feet in anger. 'You're not going to blame us! We had a very detailed brief from you. I can recall the email. In fact, I'll display it on the big screen.'

She reached for her tablet, but Penelope Abse, who had a tiny smile playing about her lips, put up a hand to stop her.

'I don't think that any of us are in doubt about Alan's role in the credits for Pony Princesses, or in its creation, come to that, but I don't see any point in digging over the past. What we all want to see is the new show. Where is it, please, Alan? We don't need a professional presentation — although yours was most impressive, Cherry, I wish my slides looked as good as that. Now, talk us through your new production, Alan, if you please.'

Alan limped on for a few more seconds, muttering about lost notes and interactivity, but as soon as it became clear that he had nothing to say, the chief executive cut him off.

'I don't propose to punish you any longer,' she said, crisply.

'The Americans loved my format,' Alan mumbled, but it was his last gasp and he sat down. He seemed to have shrunk inside his yachting blazer and his face was so pinched that he looked almost ugly.

Penelope Abse looked at Cherry.

'You have made your point, and I'm sure everyone here has noted it. May I request you to move on and show us your new format?'

'It might be better if we wait until the next commissioning meeting,' Cherry said. 'I've decided to go freelance.'

The head of the legal department shot her a swift glance.

'I think you'll find that concepts developed while you are contracted to Prize Television belong to us.'

'I'm aware of the terms of my contract, so I checked with my lawyer, and he assures me that you have no right to my original ideas, providing I develop them in my own time.'

'Possibly,' argued the lawyer. 'It depends on the circumstances.'

Cherry handed over a thick cream business card.

'Perhaps you'd like to check with my lawyer for yourself?'

The legal head read the name on the card, then did a double take.

'Tagtar Natoya is representing you?'

'Yes.'

'I'll still have to discuss the issue with him.'

The lawyer put the card in his pocket, but something about the defeated slump of his shoulders told Cherry that the battle was already won.

Penelope Abse looked directly at Cherry.

'I'm sorry to lose you, Cherry, but it's understandable under the circumstances.' Then the chief executive glared at Alan. 'You might like to consider that a more effective way of operating would have been to give proper credit to Cherry and so maintain her loyalty. You two would have made a formidable team, because, Alan, given a creative format to work with, your production skills are admirable.'

Alan looked slightly less deflated, and Cherry realised what a good manager Penelope Abse was. Alan, it was to be hoped, had learned a lesson. There was no need to humiliate him any further.

The meeting room door banged

open, and Cherish stalked in. Her eyes were red and trails of black mascara down her cheeks suggested that she'd been crying. The chief executive tactfully ignored the secretary's smeared make up, and patted the empty chair next to her.

'I'm glad to see you, Cherish. I've minuted that fact that Cherry has resigned and will be bringing her programme ideas in front of our commissioning team as a freelance in future. Perhaps you can carry on from there?'

'I'm glad she's leaving!' Cherish burst out, and all the faces in the room turned to look at her. She glared at Cherry. The secretary's eyes were almost invisible for red rims and running black mascara. 'I still want to have my say! Alan took me to France instead of you, and that shows he loves me!' She swung her face towards Alan and glared at him furiously. 'I'm not pretending any longer! Why should I keep quiet? I think you're making a fool out of me, and I won't be two-timed any longer. You can decide right now! Her or me, who's it going to be, Alan?'

Alan cast an uncomfortable glance around the room, but the scene was all his own fault, and nobody looked sympathetic. Cherry almost felt sorry for the man. At least she'd made it easy for him by retiring from the fray. He seemed to realise this, and, although he had to struggle for a minute to find it, a smile came to his face.

'Cherry will tell you that there's nothing between us.'

'Does that mean that you are committed to me?'

Alan cast an uneasy, embarrassed look at his peers. All of them were watching. Their expressions showed varying degrees and mixtures of fascination, disbelief, disgust and amusement.

'Answer me, Alan!' Cherish screamed. 'I'll never help you again if you don't. And I'll get you into trouble. See if I don't. You know I could.' Alan found his voice at once.

'Please don't be upset, Cherish. This has been a difficult time, and I admit that I've made mistakes, but you know how much our relationship means to me.'

'Where does that leave me?' demanded an angry voice.

Everyone swivelled around. Vivien stood in the meeting room doorway looking like a character in a Greek drama. She threw her head back and glared at Alan.

'You promised to marry me and be a father to my children.'

'Now Vivien, I think you were reading too much into my words . . .' Alan began.

Vivien screeched in anger. Cherish burst into tears. Penelope Abse got to her feet.

'Alan, I suggest you Vivien and Cherish clock out of work and go somewhere private to discuss your woes. Cherry, there's no point keeping you here.'

'I'll go to Human Resources and

formalise my notice,' Cherry said with a nod.

The chief executive smiled at her, then turned back to the room.

'Now, to continue . . . '

14

Luckily Cherry's position was not very senior, so she only needed to give a month's notice. Jodie from Human Resources calculated that because of leave owing and time off in lieu, Cherry only needed to work at the office for two weeks and three days before she was free.

'It'll take me that long to organise all the administrative tasks,' Cherry said, wondering what it would be like to spend all her time on productive work rather than departmental administration. Over the next week, as she tidied her desk and returned all the work that came in with a big smile and the news that it wasn't her responsibility any more, she began to wonder why she had uncomplainingly worked sixty hours a week at loathsome tasks that were nothing to do with television!

'I've been a wimp!' she told herself as she sorted, filed, and even cleaned and moved boxes.

'What on earth are you doing?' Gemma demanded.

'Archiving,' Cherry replied briefly. 'Do you think you could . . .'

Gemma flung up both hands.

'No! I absolutely refuse! You've already tried to land me with the waste contract and the vending machines. Give it to Alan! It's his job to organise the department.'

Gemma's response was echoed by most people. It's not my problem, Cherry reminded herself. It's up to Alan to make sure the administration gets done. Still, she was troubled by a nagging sense of something important remaining undone, so she made a spreadsheet, listing all the tasks that had been her responsibility. It was a ridiculously long and very mundane list. She expected she'd feel happier once she'd written out her list, but she was still troubled by the feeling that she'd forgotten something. It wasn't until her last day at work that she found out what it was.

'Look out!' Gemma hissed. 'It's the big boss, and I think she's coming here! Whatever does she want?'

Emma and Sally tried to look busy as Penelope Abse whisked in through the door. She gave a wide smile when her gaze fell on Cherry's desk.

'I've never seen your in-basket look so empty before!'

Cherry smiled back at her.

'It's been a long time since I've seen the bottom of it, that's for sure.'

The chief executive smiled again, and waved a heavyweight news magazine and a financial broadsheet.

'It's good news about your friend Edward Cameron. From what I've been hearing, he deserves all the honours that are being heaped on him.'

Cherry had to admit that she had no idea what Penelope was talking about.

'I've been too busy to read the papers,' she explained, eyeing the

316

sheaves of paper and wondering what Teddy had done to get in the news.

'I think this is the best photograph,' Penelope said, spreading the coloured magazine out on Cherry's now-empty desk top.

And there was Teddy in full colour. The photographer had managed to catch him smiling in the exuberant way that Cherry remembered so well, but there was no trace of the mad professor he had been when they originally met. He looked so handsome, so confident, so well dressed and stylish that the mist that had been clouding her brain suddenly lifted and she knew that she loved him.

'Mathematician of the Century', said the headline, and then there was a three-page article about the importance of his ideas.

Cherry couldn't speak. Now she understood why she'd been troubled with the horrible feeling that she'd overlooked something important! How could she have been so blind? How could she be so unaware of her own feelings? Why, she'd been miserable since he'd stopped smiling at her.

Penelope Abse turned the pages, and Cherry felt her heart rapping against her ribs as she looked at the photographs. There was Teddy receiving an honorary doctorate from Cambridge University. There was Teddy smiling on the steps of Number 10 Downing Street, the caption underneath explaining that he'd been invited to one of the prime minister's soirees; and there he was in a morning suit, heading for a garden party at Buckingham Palace, arm-in-arm with Harold and Angelina.

Seized with terrible anxiety, Cherry grabbed the picture and scrutinised the figures in it closely. There was no sign of Dodie, and she gave a tiny sigh of relief. But then her anxiety returned in full force. Dodie was charming and friendly, pretty and aristocratic, and she'd clearly announced her intention to marry Teddy.

'Cherry? Are you all right? Sit down!

All the colour has left your face.'

Cherry collapsed into her chair, put her hands in her mass of blonde curls and tugged hard.

'Cherry, what is it?' demanded the Chief Executive. 'Are you ill?'

Cherry lifted her head and met the kind gaze.

'No, but I think I've been out of my mind,' she murmured.

★   ★   ★

Cherry fretted and fumed through the obligatory drinks after work. The only reason she didn't walk out on her own leaving party was her uncertainty about how to approach Teddy. She wasn't sure if she had the courage to contact him. It would kill her to hear that he was falling for Dodie.

'You should be honoured, Cherry,' Gemma said, gesturing around the packed wine bar. 'Alan isn't here, nor Cherish or Vivien, but I think just about everybody else is. Even the big boss stopped by for a cocktail.'

'The people who work for Prize Television never need much of an excuse for a drink!' Cherry said.

Gemma gave her an impulsive hug.

'It's been great working with you. You'll keep in touch, won't you?'

Cherry handed out yet another of her new business cards.

'Of course I will. I'm actually going to start social networking, so you can keep track of me that way.'

Gemma kissed her.

'I'll have to go. The after-nursery club will close any minute and poor Kyle will be the last child waiting for his mummy.'

As more and more people came over to say goodbye, Cherry perversely wished they would stay, delaying the moment when she would be on her own. Soon she would have to find the courage to make a move towards Teddy.

For all her fretting, as soon as she got home to the peace of her tiny apartment, she knew what to do. She took her mobile phone over to the window so she could see the sun setting over the towers of Salford Quays. Her heart was thumping so hard she could hardly breathe.

'Harold? Hi, it's Cherry. How are you?'

They chatted for a few minutes, but Cherry was feeling so anxious that she soon blurted out, 'How's Teddy?'

'He's fine. He's fine,' Harold said, and then a pause fell. Cherry could hear Harold breathing. She held on to her phone in agony. She was convinced that Teddy was engaged and Harold was wondering how to break it to her. Finally he spoke.

'You haven't seen Teddy at all, recently, have you?'

'No,' Cherry croaked, and then she had to stop speaking. Her nerves wouldn't allow her to say another word. Her voice had let her down and her heart was hurting her. It was thudding in her chest like an enemy.

There was another, long, long pause.

'He wanted to ask you to go to Buckingham Palace with him, but he didn't want to pester you,' Harold said, and Cherry couldn't understand why his voice was so cautious.

'Pester me?' she cried, and her voice managed to both crack and squeak in only two words. She cleared her throat. 'I'd love to have gone. I want to congratulate him. I still don't understand what he did, but I do understand that he's brilliant.'

She didn't bother to go back and correct her words. After all, she was more interested in Teddy than his work, and he was brilliant, she'd just been too dull to realise it.

'That's good to hear,' Harold said, and she could hear animation in his tone. 'That's splendid, in fact. Teddy's in Majorca looking at villas. He wanted me and Angelina to join him to help him choose one, but we can't get away until Friday. I tell you what, Cherry, why don't you pop over tomorrow morning? He'd love to have your opinion.'

Cherry's leaving cocktail spun in her head, but there was no way she'd pass up this chance she was being offered. There was an urgent feeling bubbling up inside her. She had to see Teddy, but she didn't know how to make it happen.

'I could have a look on the internet for a flight, but how will I find Teddy?'

Harold laughed out loud.

'Don't be silly. Teddy sent his new jet back, so the Mustang can take you to Palma de Mallorca, then come back for us on Friday.'

A fresh wave of panic swept over her.

'I can't turn up out of the blue.'

'He'll be delighted to see you.'

Harold's tone was so warm that she had to believe him. Her brain was still telling her that it was undignified to go chasing after a man. Yet it was her heart that spoke for her.

'Then I'd love to go to Majorca.'

'That's splendid news. He'd much rather have your opinion than Dodie's. Sleep well.'

Harold rang off before she could scream at him. She collapsed limply onto her sofa, still clutching the phone. Dodie was with Teddy! They were looking at houses together! And she'd agreed to walk in on them! Harold had ruined the possibility of her getting any sleep whatsoever that night.

★ ★ ★

At sunrise the next morning, Cherry found herself being whisked through a part of Manchester Airport she'd never expected to see. The surroundings were not much smarter than the public terminals, but the service was something else. From the moment she arrived to find the uniformed plane captain waiting at the entrance for her, it was, 'Good morning, Miss Hawthorn. Let me take your bags, Miss Hawthorn. Walk this way, Miss Hawthorn.' And an unbelievable six minutes later she was boarding an elegant white aeroplane with a red stripe swooshing all the way around it. Inside the cabin of the jet aircraft was like a luxurious padded people carrier with seats for four people. It was odd to think she was the only passenger.

All the way to Majorca, Cherry was alternately thrilled to be on a private plane and terrified that she was on her way to see Teddy. She was miserably in love. She knew it was true love, the real, scary deal, and she had no idea what was going to happen when they met. She had promised to let him know if she changed her mind and wanted to spend time with him, but it was ridiculous to count on him remembering or even still feeling the same way. She remembered standing on the roof of the hotel in Blackpool, and she was sure that Teddy had been serious when he made her promise, but she also knew that people changed.

As she got off the plane the brilliant blue sky and warm, scented air couldn't cheer her. She'd been an impulsive fool.

She was met by a driver, a gloomy-looking tanned man with dark hair.

'Are you sure you are supposed to meet me?' she asked him. 'I was expecting someone else.'

His dark eyes said that he was meeting the only private jet on the tarmac, and she'd already admitted to being Cherry Hawthorn, so what on earth did she think he was doing there, but he spoke politely.

'There's no mistake, Miss Hawthorn. The Marquess of Chatburn asked me to meet you.'

Cherry opened her mouth to say 'Who?' but remembered in time that Harold's father was a duke, and so he had a title. She got into a brand-new saloon with tinted windows and shivered, because it was as cold as a refrigerator inside.

'Could you turn down the air conditioning, please?'

The driver gave her a look that said any normal person would want the air-con on full blast on such a hot day, and now he was convinced she was a lunatic, but again he spoke politely and did as she asked.

'Of course.'

And now Cherry had a new worry to ruin her trip along a winding road that took her alongside the bluest of seas and then up through fragrant green pine trees into the mountains. Why hadn't Teddy met her? Did he even know she was arriving? What if Harold hadn't told Teddy she was coming? What if Teddy was furious with her for interrupting his time with Dodie? Her mind raced and she wanted to go home.

But she didn't give the order to turn around, and after an hour driving up and ever up into the mountains, the car turned off the road, purred along a narrow track, rounded a bend and pulled to a halt in front of a circle of prickly pear bushes.

Cherry felt ill with nerves as she got out of the car. The warm air was a shock after the frigid interior of the saloon. Insects shrilled in the trees. A sharp, spicy, herbal scent teased her nostrils. She began to relax. A tiny breeze lifted her hair. The place was gorgeous; hot, calm, and quiet, apart from natural sounds like the insects buzzing in the trees and the birds whistling in the sky.

Nobody came, so the driver leaned into the car, pressing the car horn, and a klaxon blared out, shattering the sleepy afternoon.

'Don't spoil the quiet!' Cherry begged.

He gave her a look.

'We have to tell them you are here.'

Cherry walked in a circle, looking all around her.

'Where is the house?'

The driver gestured.

'There is the path, see? We will go to the house.'

He picked up her small bag before she could stop him and stumped away. Cherry had no choice but to follow his black-clad back. A pebbled path bordered by red geraniums, silvery bushes of lavender and clumps of orange marigolds led away from the parking area and between some tall cypress trees. Cherry passed along the cool shade of an aisle of tall green trees, and then the path suddenly opened out, and she could see the house.

She took in a brief glimpse of grey stone, terracotta pots of geraniums, and a large shady terrace, and then the house blurred before her because the figure of a man came around the corner of the house, shrugging into a white shirt as he walked towards her. She knew it was Teddy. Every cell in her body knew it was him.

He stopped dead, stared, then he began to run.

'Cherry!'

He raced over to her and caught her by both hands. Her heart lifted, for there, clear in his eyes, was the joy she'd been missing so badly. She could die happy now that she'd seen that expression. His face was alight with elation. She had to believe that he was pleased to see her, maybe even delighted to see her. Her breath caught, half in excitement, half in fear. She wanted to speak, to tell him how she felt, but her words caught in her throat, so she just stood, holding his hands, gazing into his happy brown eyes, letting her own eyes speak for her. How she had missed him.

The driver coughed.

'Where shall I put Miss Hawthorn's bag, please?'

Teddy turned and smiled.

'Leave it right there. I'll deal with it later.'

The driver left, and Cherry was glad to see him go, but his interruption had changed the atmosphere. When Teddy turned back to her, he was cooler, noticeably on his guard.

'Cherry, you took me by surprise, but it's very nice to see you. I'll get you a drink. Would you like to sit by the pool or inside? Or do you need to unpack first?'

'A drink by the pool,' Cherry decided.

Teddy gestured to show her the way, and side by side they walked around the corner of the house, an awkward silence between them. Cherry could feel the sunlight spilling all around them, bright in a way it never was in England. She loved the shining warmth of it. She just wished it could melt the ice between them.

'Oh!' she cried when she saw the Olympic-sized swimming pool that lay behind the villa. 'It's incredible!'

'I like it,' Teddy agreed eagerly.

The pool area was high up on a plateau. The stone was natural, and the tiles a patchwork of slate, granite and obsidian, the wet colours gleaming in the sun. Water spilled over one side of the pool, creating an illusion of infinity against the distant blue of the hills. Cherry had to walk over to the edge of the plateau to examine the view. When she looked out, she grabbed the edge of the stone wall for support.

'Whew! I'm glad there's a wall here. What a drop! What a view!'

Far in the distance was the silver drift of the sea. To one side mysterious dark mountains created a perfect balance of light and dark. The fragrance of herbs, green, spicy, warm, speaking of hot foreign landscapes, rose in the air. The generous sun seemed to make the air pulse with heat. Below them a grove of olive trees shimmered in the warmth.

'I love it here,' Teddy told her. 'Dodie keeps taking me to see new villas in the posh areas around Marbella, near the shops and the yachts, but I feel hemmed in there. I like this house, even if it is old-fashioned and out of the way.'

Dodie! Cherry felt ill at the reminder.

'Where is Dodie?' she enquired, trying to keep her tone casual.

'Shopping, and meeting friends for lunch. She gets bored up here. She says that, apart from the sun, you might as well be back in Cumbria.'

Cherry tried to take some comfort in the fact that Teddy and Dodie didn't seem to be totally compatible. If only she could ask how things stood! Teddy looked at her closely.

'You've gone pale! Come in the shade and let me get you that drink.'

Teddy might sound as if he cared about her, but the look in his eyes was still distant. She felt miserable as she followed him towards a shady area. A selection of sun-loungers stood around, and a brilliantly purple bougainvillea rambled over an arbour. He settled her into a comfortable chair, and then vanished into the coolness of the house, returning with a pitcher of fresh lemon juice and an insulated tub full of ice. Teddy sat down without speaking. Cherry took a sip of her drink, and then another, to cover the fact that she couldn't think of a single thing to say. The silence was becoming awkward.

'How have you been?' she croaked.

'Not so bad. Yourself?' Teddy muttered.

She glanced at him and then quickly away. How well he was looking! His hair looked as if he was still getting a good haircut, but today it was tousled and streaked from the sun. She was surprised by the muscles she could see in his arms and shoulders, but then she remembered his new passion for swimming. He was obviously swimming every day. He'd lost none of his freshness and individuality, but there was a new sophistication about him that suited him so well. For the life of her she couldn't speak to him.

And then they heard a distant motor engine. It grew closer. A car door slammed, there was the tap of high heels, and round the corner of the villa came Dodie. Freshly-washed dark hair spilled over her shoulders. She was wearing jeans and a shirt in her favourite crimson. She looks as if she belongs with the jet set in Marbella, Cherry thought miserably. And then she took off her sunglasses.

'Cherry?'

'Hello, Dodie,' Cherry forced herself to reply calmly.

Dodie stood stone-still for a long

second, so long that Cherry wondered if a scene was brewing.

'Well!' she drawled, finally. 'Mummy's going to be disappointed again!'

And then a big smile cracked her face, and she ran over and gave Cherry a big hug.

'It's not for want of trying, let me tell you! I've done my best to prise this gorgeous man away from you, but he's steadfast as a rock. I'm actually very glad to see you, Cherry. I don't like my friends to be miserable, and he's always going to be miserable without you.'

Teddy glared at Dodie.

'Don't ruin my strategy!'

Dodie gave him a big grin.

'You don't need it any more. It worked!'

'It did?' Teddy asked her.

'Of course it did. Cherry's come to see you, hasn't she?'

Cherry looked at Teddy.

'What strategy?'

His expression was a mixture of chagrin and glee.

'Harold advised me to play it cool.'

Cherry felt her jaw dropping.

'Edward Cameron! Have you been trying to manipulate me?'

He held out a tablet that had been lying on the table next to him and showed her what he'd been reading.

'I only acted cool because Oscar Wilde says that the affections of those we don't love are ridiculous, and I didn't want you to find me ridiculous, Cherry.'

She could see that Teddy had nearly finished the complete works of Oscar Wilde. It was difficult to be angry with a man who took your advice about what to read! He seemed to read the expression on her face and know she was softening. A laugh sprang to his eyes.

'I told you I was going to study the problem of how to mend our relationship.'

'What would you have done if I hadn't been crazy enough to fly to Majorca?'

Now he was serious.

'I would have found the answer, Cherry. If it had taken me the rest of my life, trust me, I would have found the answer.'

'Excuse me, folks,' Dodie broke in. 'When I met Carrie for lunch she happened to tell me that there's a divine French count in town. We are all invited for cocktails on his yacht at nine o'clock tonight. Will you come with me?'

Teddy and Cherry exchanged a quick glance. Neither of them wanted to go, but there was only one thing to say.

'Of course,' they said in unison.

'Then I'll go and get ready. If I can look stunning enough tonight, I may yet marry a title and make Mummy happy. It'll take us an hour to drive there, so I'll see you both at eight o'clock.'

Cherry wondered that Teddy's smile didn't split his face in half as Dodie vanished, leaving them alone. Her blood began to hum. Teddy reached out and touched her cheek with one gentle finger.

'I can't believe you're here.'

Cherry looked at his smiling face. The heat suited him, but she loved him in cool weather as well. The word 'cool' reminded her that she was cross with him.

'You didn't have to play it so cool that I missed a garden party at Buckingham Palace. Why didn't you invite me?'

'Strategy,' Teddy said, with laughing eyes. 'I wanted to, Cherry, I wanted you with me, but Harold and Angelina told me not to chase you.'

'I'll kill them!'

'Do you really want to go to Buckingham Palace with me?'

'Of course I do.'

'Well, between you, me and this sun lounger, I've been asked if I'll accept an Order of the British Empire, and I've replied to say that I'd be proud to collect it. Will you come with me?'

'I'd love to! Teddy, I've been reading

about your work. I still don't understand it, but I'm so proud of you.'

'A boring old mathematical theory? Pooh! That's not my biggest achievement. A few figures are nothing compared with the fact that you came all the way to Majorca to see me.'

She saw his eyes change as he followed the thought through.

'Does this mean that you like me?'

'Yes.'

'May I ask you how much?'

Cherry felt her heart thumping, but she owed him the truth.

'Rather a lot.'

Teddy gave his open, hearty laugh.

'Then perhaps you won't think me ridiculous if I tell you that I've loved you from the moment you stormed into the Sea View Spa and ticked me off for my parking.'

'I didn't tick you off — but you were in two spaces.' Remembering his driving she began to laugh. 'I'd never seen such a beautiful car driven so badly!'

He was laughing at the shared memory.

'I'd only picked it up that morning!'

It felt good, no it felt amazing, to be laughing and joking with Teddy again, to hear his deep laugh and see the expression in his eyes that said she was beautiful and special and funny as well. She couldn't resist teasing him more.

'Tell me you don't fly that plane of yours.'

'Not on my own, not yet, but I'm going to.'

'Are you serious?'

'Yes. I told you I was a quick learner.'

Memories came flooding back.

'Oh, it is good to see you again,' she cried.

'You, too,' he said quietly, and he reached over and kissed her.

His lips were warm and soft, and she could taste the wine he'd drunk at lunchtime.

'Although, now there's two of us . . .' His eyes were deep wells of tenderness as he glanced at her. 'And maybe more

'You are one crazy man!'

Teddy threw open his arms.

'I'm a happy man!' he corrected her, and the joy in his voice and the love in his eyes told her that he meant every word. 'Sometimes I like quiet, but other times you just have to celebrate.'

'Open the champagne,' Cherry suggested, but he surprised her again.

'Wouldn't you like a swim first?'

He gestured towards the fabulous pool with its cascades at one end and shimmering infinity horizon at the other. She suddenly realised how hot she was.

'That would be lovely. Could you lend me a . . . '

A dizzy second later she was flying through the air, and then she was in his arms and pressed lovingly to his chest.

'We don't need costumes,' Teddy said, and she could feel his deep voice rumbling in his chest.

'You can't be serious. Put me down. Teddy, I can't swim!'

'I'll support you,' he promised.

than two, I think I'll buy a bigger plane.'

'That's an excuse,' Cherry began, but then the meaning of his words hit her.

'What do you mean, more than two?'

'Wouldn't you like to have a family?'

'Well, yes, maybe, I don't know. What are you saying?'

He lifted one of her hands to his lips. His touch was so sweet.

'How do you feel about retired mathematicians?'

'I'm learning to like them,' Cherry answered with decisiveness.

'Only like?' he asked, his tone full of teasing and humour.

It was so sweet to meet his eyes and see in them the look she'd longed for: the look that said that he adored her. The look that said she was the only woman in the entire world who could make him happy.

'I love them,' she admitted.

'Enough to marry one?'

She closed her eyes for a second. She could feel her pulse drumming in her ears. The scent of flowers was so strong that it was making her feel giddy. She opened her eyes. Teddy's eyes were so loving and tender. She opened her mouth, marriage was such a huge commitment, there were so many details to discuss, but he reached out and put a finger on her lips.

'All that matters is how we feel about each other. We'll sort out the fine points as we come to them.'

Cherry surprised herself by casting caution to the winds.

'I'd love to marry you.'

Teddy's brown eyes flew open.

'You said yes!'

'Yes.'

She expected a kiss, but instead Teddy surprised her by springing to his feet.

'Mrs Cherry Cameron!' he cried, and then he executed what could only be described as a war dance. 'She's going to marry me! I'm the happiest man in the word. I feel the need for champagne, and fountains and trumpets!'

He bounded into the house, and a very few seconds later, the silvery sounds of trumpets floated over the pool.

He bounced out of the house, carrying champagne and an ice bucket.

'Verdi's triumphal march,' he told her, but he didn't sit down next to her and pour champagne, instead he skipped over to the pool shower.

Cherry sat up on her lounger and watched him. Now she could see a large chrome wheel set into the wall near the shower. Teddy turned it all the way around. She heard the sound of rushing water, and what she had taken to be a rock garden on one side of the pool turned into a series of flowing cascades. At the top of the rock pile, an enormous fountain jetted upwards. Teddy raced back to her looking pleased with the exuberance of the gushing waterfall and ringing sounds of the triumphant music.

Cherry was laughing. She couldn't help it.

Two dizzy seconds later he'd jumped off the edge of the pool with Cherry still in his arms.

Jumping into that swimming pool was like diving into champagne. She could feel his strong arms around her, and she knew she could trust him. She could feel the water, so cool and delicious, refreshing her heated skin. She could see water spraying in clear crystal bubbles in great arcs across the blue sky, and then she forgot all about the scenery because as their heads bobbed to the surface, at last Teddy kissed her.